WILL to COME Light

MYRANDA RAE

WILL COME TO LIGHT

THE UNDERWORLD DUOLOGY
BOOK TWO

MYRANDA RAE

Publisher: Myranda Rae

Publication date: April 2022

ISBN: 978-1-961031-15-9

Author: Myranda Rae

Email: connect@myrandarae.com

Website: myrandarae.com

Please direct all enquiries to the author.

ABOUT THE AUTHOR

A bonafide motha' to five kids under the age of eight, Myranda requires no fewer than 2 cups of black coffee (2 sugars) each day to support her habits and has finally built up the courage to publish her work. She enjoys noise-cancelling headphones and long waits in school pick-up lines, and can change a diaper one-handed while blindfolded.

CHAPTER 1

ane

BLOOD DRIPS from my hand down to the floor, creating a trail of my erratic movements.

Declan tries to lift his swollen face, his eyes fused closed.

"I trusted you. I left her in your care. All you had to do was drive her out of here." I grab him by his hair, yanking his head back to look at him.

I'm frantic, my heart is beating so fast I think it's going to give out. We should have had more time. I had her out in less than twenty-four hours. They should have been able to cross the border.

"We were being followed!" Oksana's voice shakes, "it's not his fucking fault."

"If either of you had anything to do with this, if you betrayed me— if you betrayed her." My voice wavers.

"I would never hurt her." Tears slip down her cheeks.

"Sir," Declan's voice is raw. "I didn't recognize any of them. I

1

killed two of the men, I'm sure they probably didn't have any identification, but maybe we could—"

"They took the bodies with them," Oksana cuts him off.

"Fuck!" I rip at my hair.

Zion steps around me, kneeling in front of Oksana to untie her hands.

"What the fuck are you doing?"

"They didn't have anything to do with this. I'm untying her." He scowls at me over his shoulder.

"One of the men had gold teeth and a tattoo on his face," she whispers to him. "A naked woman covering his cheek."

He turns to me, searching my face for recognition, but there is none.

"It's something," he pulls himself up to stand. "I'll look into it. Right now, it's the only lead we have."

"Get me a location on Farly. We're going to pay him a visit."

Zion grabs my shoulder and nods.

"All of you, get the fuck out of here."

Someone runs to grab Dec, and they all hurry to leave the room, but it's not fast enough.

"Out!" I howl as I flip my desk over. Paper and glass spray across the floor. When the door clicks closed and the last of them is gone, I truly lose control.

In a blind rage, I move through the room, breaking everything in my path. Tables, chairs, the bar, everything.

I'm a hurricane.

She might already be dead. The thought makes my stomach heave.

She didn't want to go.

I forced her to leave, and now she might be gone forever. Sometimes, living is worse than death.

Images of her—hurt, hungry, cold—flash through my mind. I wish there was more for me to break. I'm going to raise The

Underworld to the ground, scorching everything in my path until I find who is responsible for this.

This is all my fault.

My woman.

"Kane!" Zion calls, "He's at the bar."

"I'm driving. Let's go."

Whether Farly was involved is of little consequence. He threatened her. I'm taking him out, regardless.

The street is desolate. By now, word would have spread, and people are hiding. Smart.

Shooting the glass panel out of the door, I step inside. The bartender slowly raises his hands.

"He's upstairs," he gestures his head toward a door behind the bar, "but, sir, I don't think he was involved. He's been in a panic all morning."

As I round the bar and reach the door, I turn to him. "You should go."

He nods quickly and drops the glass he was washing, leaving without a second thought.

Zion is right on my heels as I climb the stairs two at a time.

"I've been waiting for this. Let's get this motherfucker!" Zion cracks the knuckles in his hands.

The sound of shattering glass as I grip the doorknob makes me smile. Please, make my day. Please be in the middle of trying to escape.

Swinging the door open with a loud bang, I immediately scan the empty office. The window is broken. It looks like the fire escape was stuck. He couldn't get the latter to release.

I turn to Zion, who is pointing up. He's on the roof.

"Go around to the other side and up," I nod to a few of my men.

"Yes, sir," they say, running quickly out of the office. We'll surround them. The roof was a particularly bad idea on their part. They're sitting ducks.

Zion's wicked smile mirrors mine. As we climb out onto the fire escape, I roll the sleeves of my shirt. I plan on getting dirty.

When I'm able to see on the roof, I can see him, surrounded by six men. He's screaming into his phone, absolutely shitting himself.

A group of several industrial air conditioning units will provide us with the perfect cover to be able to take out his entourage.

I hear the click of Zion's gun as I pull out my own. Three of my men are climbing up behind us. My seven against his six, a nearly fair fight.

This is going to be fun.

"He always has more than six people with him." I look back at my brother and guards. "You need to stay here, keeping eyes on the fire escape. I'm sure more men will be coming." I point to a guard that I normally trust. Right now everything is fucked up, and I don't trust anyone.

Zion's hand comes up to my shoulder as we turn, silently climbing over the rail. Once we're in position, calm washes over me. I don't understand feelings or softness, but I understand this. Exhaling as I squeeze the trigger, chaos erupts around us. The advantage of our position lets us take out two of his men before they can even see us.

"What the fuck!" Farly is screaming as his guards drop like flies around him.

He holds his gun out, waiting. The two men I sent around jump over the side onto the roof, taking out two more of his men. With his last two guards occupied, Zion stretches out his arm, taking aim and taking out one, leaving him and one guard. My man grabs him, holding a gun to his head while he struggles.

"I'll go grab him," Zion laughs, enjoying this thoroughly. He moves around the opposite side of the air conditioning units as I distract them.

"Farly," I yell from my covered position.

"Kane, I swear to fucking God, man. I had nothing to do with what happened." His voice shakes as he calls back to me, pleading with me.

"Tell me," I stand, meeting his gaze, "who was it then?"

"I don't know. I would fucking tell you if I knew," he grovels. Spineless little bitch.

"Get rid of him." I gesture to his guard, who is struggling against mine. With a loud pop and the thud of his body falling to the ground, Farly is alone.

"Drop the gun." I feel nothing—no adrenaline, no excitement, no fear. I'm empty.

Farly tries to get away, running directly into Zion's waiting arms. He struggles, but it's useless.

Pulling the bag from one of my men, I rummage around, I know exactly what I'm looking for.

"You see, Farly. Whether or not you were involved this morning, I'm getting pretty sick of your shit. Let's say for a moment that I believe you weren't involved. You had me ambushed not so long ago. Do you think you're fit to be king? You want my position? Think you could handle it?"

I finally find what I'm looking for, pulling it out of the bag with a twisted smile.

"Whoa, what the fuck is that?" He screams when he sees it.

"Just wait, you're going to love it," Zion laughs, "it's one of my favorites!"

"I had this bag brought in from the pits, just some toys I thought we could play with." I walk toward him as Zion wrestles him to the ground. "Do you know what this is?"

He's wide-eyed and petrified.

"This is called a knee splitter. Any guesses what it's used for?" His voice almost trembles. He's so excited.

He looks like he's ready to shit his pants or pass out, maybe both.

"That little item is from the Spanish Inquisition," Zion tells him as he forces his legs out in front of him. "They were truly ingenious when it comes to torture. Real masters of the craft."

Two of my guards come to hold his legs out straight as I slip the wooden blocks up one of his legs to his knee.

"Holy fuck, please, Kane. Please don't fucking do this!" Sweat pours from his face.

Twisting the metal rod once, the spikes inching closer together.

"Where is my wife, Farly?" I grit my teeth.

"On my life, Kane, I don't fucking know. I have my team running facial recognition. We don't know who the fuck those guys were!"

I actually believe him since our facial recognition came up empty, too.

Screwing the rod two full turns, he squirms as the spikes start to press into the front and back of his knee from both sides. It's not enough pressure to break the skin, but we'll get there.

"When you came down here, didn't anyone warn you not to fuck with Kane?" Zion taunts him, whispering in his ear.

"I didn't do it!" He screams.

"You should have taken me out when you had the chance." I force the rod around, feeling the pressure and resistance of his skin and bones as the spikes crush through. The device is completely closed, the spikes going in one side and out the other.

He screams, ear-shattering and full of anguish. The sound calms the rage in my blood. This is what I needed.

"Sir!" One of my men yells, holding out a phone to me. "You need to take this! It's about Anaïs."

CHAPTER 2

 naïs

I CAN'T SEE the clock on the console, but I know it's been hours. The driver has taken us out of The Underworld, over the bridge, through the woods, and into the great beyond.

We've passed small towns, farms, wide-open valleys, tree-packed forests, rivers, big cities, and dry, barren deserts.

I'm starting to think they don't know where they're going.

Mountain peaks are in the distance, and I groan internally. Another geographical feature to check off the list.

The closer we get, the more intimidating the mountains become. Huge reaching pinnacles stretching into the sky.

At first, the flat road starts to incline slightly, the hill growing steeper as we follow the road.

Eventually, we are driving over winding mountain roads that look out over miles and miles.

I would be awed if I wasn't waiting for my impending death. With each rotation of the tires, my hope dwindles that Kane is coming. Fear grips my heart like a fist that makes each beat painful. I'm trying not to think the unthinkable, but the thoughts won't leave me alone. They creep in no matter how hard I try to push them back.

There must be a reason he hasn't come by now. He's too hurt or he's dead. I bite into my cheek, the pain a welcome distraction from the emotions I'm barely containing.

When we turn off of the main road, the driver follows a narrow path surrounded by trees.

"We're here," Gold Teeth points to a gate in the distance.

The gate rolls open slowly, an armed guard inspecting the car before we're allowed to enter. The gravel path makes the car shake as we drive up to the largest house I've ever seen.

The monumental structure is angular, made of wood and metal, with more windows than walls.

"Come on," I'm jerked out of the car.

I'm not bound. The momentary idea of attempting escape does occur to me. It's quickly replaced with common sense, though. I'm a million miles up a mountain. I have no money or supplies. And I have no clue where I am. It's probably a bad idea.

A huge panel of glass opens, and a blonde man steps out with a huge smile on his face.

"Miss Poulain!" He takes my trembling hands in his. "I'm so happy you're here! You must be absolutely exhausted! Please, come in, let's get you settled!"

With no other options, I slowly follow him into the house.

The inside is bright white. Every single item is white or gold, it's almost blinding. I follow him into a large office, white marble everywhere.

"Is there anything you need? Can we get you anything to make you more comfortable?" The man asks, removing his pastel yellow suit jacket and sitting on a large white chair.

He gestures for me to sit. I rock on my feet, my mind racing. I expected a jail cell or a cage —something horrible.

"Um, where am I? Who are you?" Why is this guy acting like we're friends, and I wasn't just forcibly ripped away from my life?

Something flashes in his eyes as he looks at me. "I'm Gideon Cross, ruler and King up top." His voice is clipped, the cheerfulness it held only a moment ago is gone. I think I offended him by not immediately recognizing him.

"Why am I here, Mr. Cross? Why did you kidnap me?"

He gasps, "We didn't kidnap you! We rescued you!"

"Rescued me from what?"

"From Kane Azrael!" He's looking at me like I'm an idiot.

"I didn't need to be rescued from Kane. It didn't feel like a rescue, there was a car chase and shooting, and my friends were held at gunpoint..."

"We were trying to separate you from your captors! You were never in harm's way! The whole point was to keep you safe!"

"I didn't feel safe. It felt like I was being kidnapped." I'm still so confused. "Kane isn't holding me captive? Why would you think that?"

"I'm so sorry. I thought you were being held there against your will. It's inconceivable to me that someone would willingly choose to stay in The Underworld."

"Right, well, I did choose to..." my voice dies in my throat. "What do you mean to choose to stay in The Underworld?"

"You know," he shrugs, "it's just surprising. We've never heard of a case like yours. I didn't even consider that you would want to stay there. I mean no offense, but it wasn't even in the realm of possibility."

I'm trying to piece together what he's saying, but it's as if I don't understand the words. Everything is jumbled up.

"By 'want to stay there' you mean what, exactly?"

"I mean, when it was discovered that you were an innocent who was never convicted of a crime, you should've been sent back up top where you belong. When he told you that they would be arranging transport for you to come here… you chose not to accept it."

The room spins, and I sink into the seat. His words boom in my mind so loudly that they rattle my brain.

"It's illegal for you to be here without a conviction. You could be sent to the pits…"

He lied to me. No. No, he didn't. Kane wouldn't lie to me.

"He… he told me it was illegal for me to be down there."

"That's true. It is illegal for someone who hasn't been convicted of a crime to be in The Underworld."

I sigh, relieved.

"But," he continues, "the remedy for that would be to send that person, you, up top."

"I don't believe you."

He laughs in my face, holding his stomach like I've just told the best joke he's ever heard. When he finally stops laughing, he has so much pity in his eyes.

"You don't have to believe me, but it is the truth. What reason would I have to lie to you? By the look on your face, I can surmise that he didn't inform you of your right to choose. You can say whatever you want, but your eyes give you away."

"I won't believe it until I can talk to Kane. You said you didn't kidnap me. I want to speak to him." I sit up straight, hoping to look more confident in my demands.

"I'll do you one better." He stands and walks towards his desk, pressing a button on the phone.

"Angelica, call Kane Azrael. Set up a meeting at his earliest convenience. Tell him Miss Poulain would like to see him."

"Yes, Sir, right away."

"Thank you, Angelica."

He turns to me with a smile on his face. "We'll have a little face-to-face."

My heart races. He's still alive. A weight is lifted from my chest, and I can finally breathe. I just have to wait until he gets here, then everything will be alright. He wouldn't lie to me.

"If I wanted to leave and go back to him right now, you would let me." I'm still not convinced that I'm not actually being held here.

"Absolutely, you're not a prisoner. You can choose whatever you want and it will be respected."

He's trying to turn me against him. I won't fall for it.

"Anaïs, may I ask you something?"

I nod.

"I understand that you were frightened this morning by our covert efforts to get you out of The Underworld, but you still look frightened. You're not afraid of me, are you? I have no reason to harm you."

I don't know what to say. When I look at him, I don't feel fear. He looks so...harmless. If he's Kane's enemy, then he's mine. I just need to keep his voice out of my head long enough for Kane to arrive.

CHAPTER 3

ane

It feels like we're moving in reverse. We should be there by now.

The torture that I'm going to rain down on Gideon hasn't even been thought of yet. I'm going to invent something special, just for him.

None of this makes sense. Why would he go to all the trouble of taking her, only to call me a few hours later and arrange for me to come to get her?

"Ok, look," Zion has wanted to say something for the past several hours but he's held back. "I'm just going to say this, and you can take it or leave it, but... I think it needs to be said. Something is fucked about this. You can feel that, right? We need to be prepared for what we're walking into."

"I assume this is some kind of trick, a ploy to draw me out of The Underworld or an attempt to kill me, I don't know, but I can't *not* go. Anais is there, she's waiting for me. I have to go, even if it's a trap."

"Sir," the driver calls, "we're here."

My chest is so tight that I can't inhale as the car stops in front of a gate.

If a single hair on her head is so much as out of place, I will turn the entire world into Hell.

"Mr. Azrael," A guard steps forward, "we're going to need to search you and hold any weapons here at the security outpost."

Stepping out of the car, I let him pat me down. Zion is behind me mumbling under his breath about Gideon being a little bitch.

"All I'm saying is, we don't confiscate his weapons when he's in The Underworld. He's a pussy, end of story."

"Zion, shut the fuck up." I can't take anymore. Nothing is moving. The car is slow, the gate is slow, the fucking guards are slow. Everything is trying to stand in the way of me getting to her.

I'm out of the car before it's stopped, Zion rushing out behind me. I can't wait another minute to see with my own eyes that she's alright. Deep down, in a place I'm trying not to think about, the thought crossed my mind that she's not alight, that she's dead and this is a trick.

The door opens just as we reach it, and Gideon steps out.

"Oh, fuck!" I barely register Zion's voice. I've got Gideon by the throat, pressing him into the glass.

"Where is she?"

He makes a gurgling sound as Zion pulls a concealed knife from his belt and holds it to the throat of the nearest guard.

"Whoa, back the fuck up," he growls as the team that runs out to free Gideon.

He chokes, trying to talk or even breathe against the pressure of my hand.

"Kane?"

Anaïs.

I drop him, coughing and stuttering on the ground. I turn to see her running toward me.

"Baby," I whisper into her hair as I hold her. She curls into me and her shoulders shudder.

I'm shattered. I can't breathe. If Gideon wanted to kill me, now would be the time. I feel everything at once, burning in my blood, a rolling, rapid churning that drains me.

I want to kill everyone... to kiss her and hold her and fuck her. I won't be whole until she's wrapped around me until I'm so deep inside of her that we can't be separated. I need to show her, to love her, to make her feel me.

Everything around us is static, white noise that I can barely hear.

"I apologize for this horrible misunderstanding, Kane," Gideon is dusting off his piss-colored pants. I need to get her away from here right now.

"I hope you can understand my position. I'm sorry for the inconvenience this caused and the fear that everyone felt. I thought I was rescuing her..." He continues. I know where he's going with this. Mother fucker. Taking her hand, I turn to walk toward the car, but she's standing firm, watching me.

"Kane, wait," her voice is so soft and small that I almost don't hear it.

Fuck. Fuck. Fuck.

She knows. He already told her. I underestimated him. Everything is suddenly crystal clear. He's not going to hurt her, not physically, anyway. He told her the truth, and now he's going to let me drown. He's ripping her away from me using my own stupid fucking lie.

"I... Anais," I weigh my options. If I tell her he's lying, she might believe me. I can cover this, Zion will back me up. I can't lie again.

"Can we talk, inside?" I can see how nervous she is, nervous to talk to me.

"Use my office." Gideon is being so friendly and helpful I want to rip his tongue out. He's tearing my life apart with a smile on his face.

When we're alone, I reach for her, longing for the feeling of her body pressed to mine. She lets me hold her, her arms wrapping around my waist. She's alive, she's safe, she's going to fucking leave me. I should be grateful that she's letting me touch her at all after I sent her away.

"Kane," she steps back after several minutes of silence, just standing there staring at me with those big eyes. The sadness there is like physical pain. I have to rub my hand over my chest to try to stop the hurt radiating there.

She's just standing there watching me waiting for me to explain. I can see it in her face, she's teetering on a thin ledge between heartbreak and hope. Even now she still believes in me she still holding onto that tiny thread of hope that this is a misunderstanding and I didn't lie to her. All I have to do is tell her, and she'll believe me.

"It's true." I hardly recognize the sound of my voice.

The broken gasp that heaves from her chest and the way she steps back slightly, as if I physically hit her, nearly kill me.

Her eyes well up instantly, and huge tears roll down her soft cheeks.

"So when you said it was illegal for me to be there..."

I cut her off. "That's true. It is illegal for you to be there."

I'm grasping at straws here, trying to minimize the lie.

"It is illegal for you to be there because you were not convicted of a crime. You should have been sent back up top." I think my heart might've stopped beating.

"Why did you lie to me?" The hurt is so sharp in her voice that it feels like it's cutting into my chest.

"I didn't want you to go. It was for my own selfishness. The moment I saw you, I wanted you. I wanted you to be mine, no matter what your crime was. When I discovered you had committed no crime I couldn't let you leave. So you lied to me you." I can't breathe.

"You told me that you would be devoted to me and that I would be your partner—your equal, but you lied!"

Fuck. It's like I swallowed razor blades.

"Yes."

There's nothing else to say.

CHAPTER 4

 naïs

I FEEL PHYSICALLY ILL. I'm standing in front of the only man I've ever trusted while he admits that our entire relationship has been based on lies. If he had told me the truth, I would have picked him.

I feel like I'm underwater, sinking further and further below the surface.

"I-I need a minute," I push past him and run down the shiny white hallway. Alone in the pristine bathroom, everything crashes down around me. Every single moment we've spent together runs through my head. Images of his skin, his hands on my body, his lust-filled eyes... what usually makes my body pulsate with need makes my stomach roll.

I hear his shoes, the tick of his steps against the ground. I know he's outside the door, so I cover my mouth with my hands. I don't want him to hear my crying.

I feel so betrayed.

My father expected absolute silence. I was to cook, clean, and care for him without letting anyone know I existed. We never talked, he never asked me what I liked, or what I wanted from my life.

My favorite time of day was just after dark. He always stepped out, enjoying the excessive pleasures that The Underworld offers. I was left alone, free to dream and imagine a life far away.

Kane was like a tidal wave that came and swept me away. He brought me into his life, placed me beside him, and made me feel like there was no dream too far out of reach. It was all a lie. His words are pretty, but they don't mean anything. Not when his actions don't match.

He wants to control me, to force me, to bend me to his will. He lied, and he sent me away. He's just like my dad, he only hides it better, which might be worse.

Every second I spend in the bathroom, my anger grows.

I gave him everything. I bet he's out there right now, thinking that I'm about to come out and forgive him.

Ripping the door open, I step out, and he jumps up from the bench against the wall.

"Anaïs -"

I put my hand up and his mouth snaps shut.

"I used to read a lot when I lived with my dad. There wasn't really much else for me to do since I had to be quiet." He looks confused.

"Maya Angelou, have you read any of her work?"

He nods.

"After I read her books, I was so enamored with her that I looked up everything I could about her. There is a quote from her that always kind of stuck with me. 'When someone shows you who they are, believe them.' I always thought it was so simple yet truly brilliant."

He takes a step toward me, but I back away, just out of reach.

"You've shown me who you are. Your words and your actions don't match up. I gave you things I can never get back, Kane." I don't mean to let tears fall, but they slide down my cheeks, too heavy to hold back. He has my body, my soul, my heart.

"Fuck, baby, please," his voice wavers, "I'm so sorry. I know it was wrong. I just didn't want you to leave."

"Don't you think I should be with you because I want to be? Doesn't it bother you that I'm there under false pretenses? You're sorry now, but that's only because I found out the truth. If Gideon hadn't come for me, I would be at the beach house right now... Would you have told me the truth, ever?"

He runs his hand over the back of his neck and sighs. His silence is deafening.

"I didn't want you to find out. When I lied... I didn't understand... I just knew I wanted you. I didn't know what you would become. Then, once I realized that I can't live without you, I kept it from you because I thought that this," he gestures between us, "would happen."

"I'm not a possession. You don't get to lie and withhold, command, and dictate to keep me."

An angry, humorless laugh scratches at my raw throat. "You know, before I met you, I would never have had the nerve to stand up for myself. I guess you did give me that. Do you wish you hadn't?"

"No, I'm proud of you. You don't deserve a King that lies to his Queen."

We stand in silence, my throat aching with the pressure of the tense lump I'm forcing down.

"Are there any other lies?"

"None." I might be the stupidest woman that ever lived, but I believe him.

"I need time, Kane. I..." my voice cracks and I have to stop to collect myself.

19

"You can stay at the beach house. I'll give you all the time you need. I can send Oksana and Jiji. I won't bother you. I still need to know that you're safe."

My heart clenches. Oksana and Jiji are alright.

I nod, I won't be able to hold back sobs if I open my mouth. It would be less painful to stab myself through the heart than to keep looking at his sad face. He looks like he doesn't know what to do.

With trembling steps, I run to him, wrapping my arms around his chest. He inhales sharply as he pulls me towards him.

This is wrong. It's torture for both of us but he is my greatest comfort.

What a twisted turn of events that the reason I need comfort is because of him. Somehow, he is both the pain and the remedy.

He doesn't speak, just holds me tightly with one arm while the other runs through my hair.

"I don't want you to leave," he finally breaks the silence.

"I don't want to leave. I just need space to think. If I don't separate myself from you, I'll forgive you by tomorrow. I need more time."

Ragged sighs slip past his lips as we stand, clinging to each other. I know I need to go, I need to find a way to comfort myself. Letting him ease the pain will only make it more difficult to leave.

"If you need anything, will you call me?" He whispers softly into my hair.

"Yes."

"Oksana will be at the house when you arrive." His chest tenses, squeezing me tighter as if he can sense before I do it, I'm about to pull away.

I force myself out of his arms, walking away without looking back.

CHAPTER 5

 ane

I'M HOLLOW. It's been five days, or five months, or five centuries, time doesn't matter. Nothing matters.

I'm a ghost, cursed to roam the empty halls of my lonely world alone.

I knew what I had and, somehow, didn't. I knew this would hurt. I was aware my world was crumbling around me, but the full extent couldn't be realized until I came home without her.

Her giggle, the easy way she walks, light and graceful across the floor, her voice, her sighs, her clothes on the bedroom floor. It's like I see her moving in the shadows, taunting me. She's here, she's everywhere, but I can't touch her.

Sleep is torturous. If I manage to force myself to drift off, she haunts me. Every moment of sleep is spent in restless agony. I wake covered in sweat, reaching out for her.

Sighing, I pull myself out of my big empty bed. Walking through the desolate halls of my house I can't help the gnawing ache that presses against my chest. The unwelcome memories play in my mind on an unending reel.

Last week, I came home from a meeting to find Anaïs and Oksana dancing in the kitchen. There were dirty pots and food everywhere. They were attempting spaghetti. Jiji was nipping at their ankles and barking as they screamed out the lyrics to a song that I don't know and can't remember now.

My house has never known laughter or fun. I've never come home to happy squealing and off-key singing before.

The memory makes me smile while it simultaneously rips my heart out. Everything is darker now.

Spreading the plans across my desk, I sink into my chair. Mercy Fields. I keep putting off making decisions about this. I want her here. Construction to begin leveling the ground will start next week. There are so many small details that need to be settled, I just can't bring myself to do it.

"Kane?"

I groan and drag myself out into the hallway.

"Why are you here?" I don't have the energy for Zion right now.

"It's been almost a week, man. You should come to The Playground, and take your mind off of things. She's not the only tight pussy in The Underworld. Shake it off, get your dick wet."

Blinding rage takes over and I swing before he's finished speaking. When my fist connects with his face he turns to me, smiling.

"There he is," his grin widens as he steps forward, pressing all of his weight into his fist as he uppercuts me.

We circle around the living room, hands up, guarding our faces.

Lunging forward, I fake a right hook that he blocks, but my left jabs forward, clipping his chin.

"Fuck," he chuckles as he moves his jaw before striking out, throwing several punches. I block most of them, but he lands a few which adds to my fury.

"Come on, big brother, your reflexes are getting a bit slow," he taunts as he side-skips just beyond my reach.

Reaching forward, I grab his collar in my fist, pulling him forward. He screws his face up, ready for impact. Two quick punches and I drop him back, pushing him, giving myself time to guard my face.

"How's that for slow reflexes? Fucker."

He tips his head back and laughs, blood dripping down his face, "I guess I misjudged the fight you still have in you. Truce?" He extends his hand.

"Yeah, whatever." I turn to sit on the stairs but he sucker punches me in the stomach.

I've had enough of his shit. Still hunched over, I lunge forward, tackling him to the ground. We haven't fought like this since we were kids.

We struggle, rolling over each other, throwing elbows and as many punches as we can.

By the time we've finished, we're covered in blood and sweat and some of my furniture is broken.

"What the fuck is wrong with you?" I pour us each a shot of whiskey.

"You've been mopey as a motherfucker the past five days. My big brother doesn't take shit lying down. If you want her, and your reaction tells me you do, go get her. Why aren't you up top fighting for her?"

Gulping down the warm liquid, I pour another shot.

"She wants space, time away from me."

"It's been five days. That's plenty of time. Go get her. Tell her that you fucked up and fix it." he slides his empty glass toward me.

"It's not that easy. I bulldozed her into doing what I wanted

her to do before. She has to come back when she wants to. If—"
My heart hurts, "if she wants to."

"Does she know how you're feeling? Have you talked to her?"

"Fuck, listen, you're trying to be helpful, I think, but this is beyond your depth. Hell, it's beyond my depth. I'm doing the opposite of what I would normally do."

I want to go to her, to drop to my knees before her, to show her how I feel the only way I know how. To love her body until she understands, until there are no doubts in her mind that I'm sorry.

"You're not going to her because you want to go to her?" His brow quirks. "Relationships are confusing as fuck. That's why I hit it and quit it, man."

"When I tell someone to do something, I expect it to be done. When someone lies to me, when they try to manipulate me, that's it. I've killed for less. My woman deserves at least that much. It's the lowest possible standard that I can hold myself to, to be truthful with her."

"What if she doesn't come back?" I know he's asking legitimate questions, one I've asked myself countless times in the past four days, but it knocks the air out of my lungs.

"If she decides she doesn't want to come back, I have to let her go. I can't force her. As long as she's happy and safe, I can learn to live with that."

He nods his head, "I don't understand wanting to be with only one person, but... I think for you... it's a good look. You're still an asshole but you're slightly less of a miserable prick."

CHAPTER 6

 naïs

THE LOUD ECHO of the doorbell breaks the silence of the morning.

Jogging toward the door I'm expecting fruits and flowers. Every morning there is a delivery—a massive bouquet of flowers and a different kind of delicious, ripe fruit.

Kane.

I look forward to it every day. It's the one bright spot in my life right now. It's not as good as seeing him but it's something.

It's not manipulative or intrusive; he just cares. It's his way of taking care of me while he gives me the space I need.

Pulling the door open, I'm surprised to see Zion standing outside on the front stairs. He has a black eye and stitches on his cheek.

Oh, no. My heart lurches in my chest.

"What happened? Is he alright?"

"Well, physically, he's fine, mostly," he runs one hand over the bruised knuckles on the other.

"I've come to talk to you on my brother's behalf..." He looks nervous?

"Why did he send you? Why didn't he just come to talk to me himself?" I find myself feeling irritated. Kane isn't the type to send someone else when he wants something. I asked for space, sending Zion isn't any better than coming himself. In fact, it's worse.

"He didn't send me. He doesn't know I'm here. Are you going to forgive him, Anaïs?" In true Zion fashion, he jumps right to the point.

"I'm just taking some time away. He broke my trust..."

"He'll kick my ass for telling you this but... he's fucking miserable..."

I cut him off. "I'm miserable too! He did this, Zion! I'm not up here because he forgot to put the toilet seat down! Our entire relationship was based on deception. If he had told me the truth, I would have picked him, I would have stayed with him. I hate it here. I miss him every minute. I just need time. If I go back to him right away... he can't ever do this to me again. I need to know that he'll be honest...that he won't keep things from me or..."

"Whoa, whoa," he holds his hands up, stopping my increasingly frantic ranting. "I'm not saying that you're not miserable too... but..." he rubs his hand over the back of his neck. "If you're both so unhappy, why not just, fix it? Fuck, I don't know! I don't know about this shit."

"Zion, I'm scared," the words come out shuttering and broken. "What if everything was a lie? What if I come back and he does it again? I... I love him." a sob rips at the back of my throat.

He sighs and looks at the ground. "Fuck." He scrubs his hand over the back of his neck. "Look, He's all fucked up. I can't speak for him... you need to talk to him. He's trying to give you space and respect what you asked, so he's not going to call you. He won't come here. It's killing him, but he's staying away."

I open my mouth to speak, but a whimpering sound is all that comes out.

"Shit, please, stop crying." He looks so uncomfortable that even in this emotional state, it makes me want to laugh.

"Sorry," I sniffle and try to stop myself. He looks so similar to Kane that it's difficult to even stand in front of him.

"He won't come because he loves you, too. If you want to live up here, if it's what you really want, he won't beg you to come back. Not because he isn't dying without you, but because he wants you to be happy. Even if it's at the expense of his own happiness..."

His words cut into my chest like knives.

"Zion," Oksana's voice calls from the stairs, "she's not ready to hear this."

He sighs and shrugs his shoulders. "I don't know what the fuck I'm doing. I'm just trying to help."

"Thank you," I try to smile but my lips turn down. "Will you just... take care of him for a little while longer?"

"Of course," he nods, "I'll just keep kicking his ass until he comes to his senses."

"Wait! Did he bust up your face like that?" My gaze goes immediately to his knuckles again.

"Yeah, but you should see him!"

I cringe at the thought of cuts and bruises on his handsome face.

The doorbell rings, and I'm grateful for the distraction. My fruit and flowers. The delivery man hands me a huge bouquet of orange and purple blooms with large, waxy leaves. I've never seen a flower quite like it. The petals are like spears, long and thin with pointed ends.

"Birds of Paradise," he gestures to the flower, "we've gone to the tropics today, the fruit is mango."

I take the items and close the door, leaning against it to pull myself together.

I hear a squeal from upstairs just before the door slams shut. I guess Zion's agenda included more than just talking to me.

Setting my gifts on the counter in the kitchen, I take Jiji out onto the large patio. Staring out at the water, I take a deep breath. I haven't been able to walk on the beach yet. So far, my time here has been spent exclusively missing Kane. He's taken up permanent residence in my brain. It's not easy to think and get clarity when I can't even take a shower without blushing.

Every part of this house is filled with memories that slap me in the face all day long.

"Come on my sweet boy," now is as good a time as any to get over being on the beach without him. We had our first kiss here. I stare at the sand where we stood. His fingers slid into my bikini and touched me, his tongue massaging mine. Then watching him in the shower...

I miss him.

Sighing, I walk through the warm sand. Maybe I should just go home.

CHAPTER 7

 naïs

WALKING ON THE BEACH, just as I suspected it would, made everything jumbled up in my head. My whole body hums, missing his touch by the time I get back to the house.

I'm doubting myself. Is this whole thing a stupid overreaction that is just torturing both of us for no reason?

My skin feels salty and dry from hours under the sun.

Creeping into the house, I bring Jiji upstairs. I've been sleeping in the same room I stayed in when we came here. Instead of going to my floor, I go to his. Everything inside the room looks exactly the same.

With us, so much has changed but also not so much.

I'm here, upset at him for making a decision for me, which is what he tried to do last time.

He's the king in The Underworld. The most powerful man I've ever met. He isn't used to asking, or considering the opinions of others. I truly believe that he's trying.

Am I being blinded by the way he makes me feel? Am I making excuses for an established pattern of behavior because I miss him?

Because, damn, do I miss him.

I find myself being whishy-washy, hoping he'll show up, even being disappointed when he doesn't. I told him not to. I told him I needed time and space. He's respecting me, thats what I want.

But I also want him.

Stepping into his shower, I groan at the memories this room holds. His big hands wrapped around his even bigger....

His face.

His wet skin.

His broad shoulders.

His muscular chest.

A hot, sticky, hammering between my legs has me doubting everything.

Turning off the water, I slip into one of his shirts just as I have every night. His smell is so faint that it's hard to catch it at all but it's better than nothing.

"Zion wanted to say bye," Oksana looks up when I enter the kitchen. She has limes and ice and different bottles of alcohol out on the counter. "Does he have a blender? I'm making margs!"

After searching the entire kitchen, we find it in the pantry.

"This will fix you right up," she smiles, handing me a slushy, pale green drink.

Taking a sip, then a slightly bigger gulp, I sink into one of the barstools.

"You don't like it?"

"Oh, no, it's really good. I'm just thinking..." Thinking about Kane, wondering what he's doing right now. What he's wearing... if he ate today...is he getting any sleep?

"Have you thought about calling him?" She tops off my glass with the leftovers from the blender.

"Basically every minute since I got here." It's embarrassing how true that actually is.

"What's holding you back?"

"I'm afraid that he won't take me seriously. I'll come back to him and in no time, we'll fall right back into this pattern. I don't want the same kind of life I had with my dad. It turned out to be an illusion, but I thought we had that... a real relationship with respect and honesty."

"Well," she sits in the seat beside me, "if it means anything. I think this is a good thing. He should have to sweat for a little while."

"It's starting to feel like I'm punishing myself."

"Stay strong, girl," she starts cutting and peeling one of the mangoes.

"Easy for you to say," I snort, "your guy just left."

She blushes deep red, "whoa whoa whoa... not *my* guy... a guy... just a guy."

"Sure, right, of course."

"Zion isn't the type to settle down."

I search her face for sadness but there isn't any.

After a few minutes of eating the delicious sweet fruit, she starts to chuckle to herself.

"He's not the type to settle but the dick is immaculate!" She shivers and a mischievous smile spread across her face.

"Oh, geez. Let's not talk about that...immaculate dicks..." I blush furiously, "that's not helpful."

Her head falls back and a loud, joyful laugh fills the air. I'm so happy she's here with me. She's been giving me space. We haven't really talked about Kane. It might be the alcohol in this drink, but I'm feeling loose.

"Do you think I'm overreacting?"

"No," she stops laughing and nods her head adamantly. "You're not."

"I keep wavering, doubting myself..."

"Can I be honest with you?" She gulps down the rest of her drink.

"Of course."

"I've been thinking about this... He was wrong, he lied but," she stops like she's not sure she should continue.

"But..." I chuckle, waiting.

"But... I don't think he was malicious. Do you? A lie is a lie..."

"That's what I'm struggling with. I keep thinking about him, about his personality and his history. He doesn't know how to do relationships. He knows how to rule and command and do what it takes to ensure things go his way... I don't want to make excuses for him but I'm finding it hard not to." I rub my hands over my tired eyes. "He said he wants me to be his equal and in some ways he has treated me that way...I don't want to excuse lying or demanding but that is who he is. I can see how, at the time, he didn't think what he was doing was out of line. When he did realize it, he didn't know how to fix it."

She just sighs and shrugs.

"Or maybe he's a lying liar." I lay my cheek against the cool countertop frustrated and exhausted from the never-ending thoughts in my head.

"I should just call him." "Girl, you should call him." We both speak at the same time.

"I think that's a sign." She laughs. "You go call. I'll make more drinks!"

My palms are sweaty as I walk upstairs to make the phone call. I find myself absentmindedly fixing my hair, even though he won't be able to see me.

"Kane, I just wanted to call..."

"Kane, It's Anaïs !"

"Hey, it's me, I'm calling to chat…"

Why does everything sound so stupid and unnatural? I've talked to him plenty of times. I should know how to do this.

Sitting in the middle of the bed, I hold the phone in my hand like it's a snake that's about to bite me. I know hearing his voice is going to affect me. Taking a deep breath, I hit the button to call and wait, my heart pounding.

Voicemail.

My heart sinks, and I have to throw the phone to stop myself from immediately redialing. I need another drink.

CHAPTER 8

 ane

"KANE," she whispers in the dark, "I need you."

I'm instantly hard. Reaching for her body in the bed, she's beside me. My heart beats so hard it hurts. She's here.

I run my hands over her, feeling all the soft skin I've missed so desperately.

"I missed you," she whispers, crawling over the bed to lie on top of me.

"You will never leave me again," I groan against her mouth. "I won't give you a reason to."

"Kane, please," her voice is breathy and soft, "I need you, please. I missed you so much."

My body burns, my skin, my lips, my hands... I ache to touch her.

Her fingers reach out of the dark, running down my chest. Having her so close, the crack in my chest starts to heal. The hollow pit that's grown each day that she was gone, starts to repair itself.

Rolling on top of her, I stare down at her face. The face I've missed every day. Her smooth skin is tan from the sun up top, new freckles are scattered across her cheeks.

Her fingers graze my face, running back into my hair and down to my neck.

"Goddammit," the weight in my chest dissolves into a new kind of pain. The deep, endless pain that walks hand in hand with love. Now that I know equally well what life can be like with her and without her, love is no longer soft. There is something sharp about it, something threatening. If I ever fuck up again, I know the genuine anguish that awaits if she leaves.

The blunt tip of my cock presses against the soft, wet entrance to her flawless cunt. Stopping to take a breath, I have to fortify myself before pressing forward. I've missed her so much. I've been lost without her.

"I have so many things I want to say," I groan, dropping my forehead to hers, "I don't know how…"

"Show me, baby," she whispers. "If you can't find the words, show me." As it always is, her touch brings calm to my chaos.

With a strained moan, I push the tip into the maddening tightness between her legs. My second home, my place of worship.

Her back arches toward me, inviting me in, sucking my soul straight through my cock.

"Fuck, it's so much better than the dreams," I slide into her, the slickness of her clenched walls luring me in while also pulsating, to push me out. Goddamn, it's so fucking good.

I move slowly, rocking into her, losing myself in her.

The little moans and sighs she makes are working me into a frenzy. I want to love her more, harder, deeper. Not to fuck her, but truly adore her. I want to touch her heart, to be so deep inside of her that she can feel the immeasurable, bottomless need I have for her.

I'm not deep enough, it's never enough.

Physically, it feels so good I'm lightheaded. Emotionally, it hurts, aching and churning in every part of me.

A tortured sound rips at my throat as I look down at where we connect. My cock slides into her, covered in her delicious, glistening wetness.

"Kane, oh my... *god,*" her breathless voice begging me. Her arms wrapped around me. Her hands on my back—her body arching forward into mine. I've never been this hard. Instinctually, I want to pound into her, to fuck her so hard she'll feel me between her legs for days, but I don't. This isn't fucking, not tonight. This is offering praise at the altar, revered and devoted.

I will show her—prove it to her. I don't deserve her and I'll never forget it. She won't ever doubt how much I need her or that she rules me—owns me.

Running my fingers over the soft curve of her neck, committing every inch of skin to memory, I move down over the swell of her breasts, to her stomach. When I reach the soft, wet skin between her legs, I rub circles against her clit.

I can't come yet but she can and she will, over and over again.

Her body tenses, tightening around me. Words fail me. Strangled moans and grunts, that's all I can manage. With each rolling motion of my hips, I'm closer to nirvana, the bursts of pleasure pinging all over my skin.

She comes, once, twice, three times as I fuck her, bringing myself to the edge, then holding back.

When she finally screams my name, loud, aching, broken, I know her body can't handle much more.

"I'm coming, baby," pressure builds, my vision is blurry, and my body aches.

"Baby," she sighs, her voice is far away...

"Anaïs?" I reach for her, grabbing at her skin, but she's sinking into the sheets.

Jolting upright in the inky darkness, I choke, coughing and heaving, my chest collapsing.

I'm soaked in sweat, my cock so hard it hurts.

"Fuck!" I scream into the empty bedroom.

She's not here. Of course, she's not.

She left me.

The Underworld is my home, it's my kingdom. I never saw my place here as a punishment or a curse, but rather as a position of respect. Right now, I *feel* eternally damned. My soul is lost in the abyss. She brought a light into my world that leaves behind a dark mass as it fades away. I'm falling into a black hole.

I deserve this. I can't be ruler here, punisher, executioner, reaper, and still have her. Her tender heart in my rough hands is dangerous. It's vile. I corrupt her. Her words play in my mind, "*I gave you things I can't get back.*"

She hasn't called. Of course, she hasn't.

The allure of the bright, warm sun and crystal water are replacing any thoughts she has of me.

Fisting my swollen, angry cock in my hand, I go through the motions. The physical reaction to stimulations takes over and the misery in my mind is pushed down long enough to come in spurts over my stomach.

Pulling my battered body from my bed, I move into the bathroom. Avoiding my gaze in the mirror, I shave the overgrown stubble from my face, then shower.

With forced determination and simmering rage, I pull on a suit.

"Look alive." I step out into the living room, surprising Declan. "We're going into the office today."

His coffee sloshes out of his cup onto his hand. If it burns, he doesn't show it. He hasn't seen me since my scuffle with Zion. He doesn't ask about the deep blue bruises. Not that I would answer if he did.

CHAPTER 9

 naïs

I CALLED four times during the night, but he never answered. I would have called fifty times but I thought fifty missed calls was a little bit excessive.

I didn't sleep for a single minute. I'm exhausted and frustrated by the time I make it downstairs.

"Well?" Oksana looks at me expectantly. After he didn't answer the first time, we drank several more of her boozy creations. My alcohol-soaked brain, nerves, and lack of sleep are joining forces to swirl together into a nauseous pit in my stomach.

"He never answered," I sink down to sit on the bottom step.

"Really?" She looks nervous too, which adds to my panic.

"Can you try calling Zion? Just to check to make sure that everything is okay..." I'm trying to stay calm. Maybe everything is completely fine and he's ignoring my calls on purpose. That would be better than some of the alternatives that have crept into my mind in the darkness of night.

"I'll call him right now," she places the phone down on the counter, the trilling sound of the ring filling the quiet room. I can't breathe.

When the voicemail message starts to play her face drops.

"Ok, let's not panic. If one of them isn't answering, it's not unreasonable that the other doesn't answer. They are usually together... maybe they are both just busy."

Yeah, busy being attacked and killed.

"I'm going to call Gideon. He gave me his phone number before I left his house, maybe he knows what's going on."

Running upstairs, I search my bedroom to find the slip of paper with his number on it. I almost threw is away, I'm glad I didn't. My whole body trembles, a thousand horrible scenarios playing out in my head— ambushes and injuries, attacks and gun battles.

The shakiness of my fingers makes it hard to dial the number. My breath catches as it rings.

"Hello?" Why does his voice always sound so cheerful?

"Good morning, Mr. Cross, it's Anais," I try to make my voice sound normal.

"Anaïs! Good morning, please, call me Gideon. To what do I owe the pleasure of this call?"

"I'm so sorry to bother you so early in the morning, but I was wondering if you had heard anything about The Underworld." This was such a stupid idea. "Is there something going on?"

"Oh please, don't be silly, you're not bothering me at all! I haven't heard anything..." He doesn't skip a beat.

I pause for a moment. Am I really about to ask him to do this?

"Um, would you do me a favor?" I chew my lips. Yes, I guess I am asking him to do this.

"What do you need?" I listen closely to his voice, searching for anything hidden there, annoyance, amusement, judgment. There is nothing.

"Can you call Kane? Just to check? I—just—"

"Sure, give me a minute. I'll call you back."

"Thank you." I don't know why asking him to do this is so difficult.

Jiji sits beside me on the bed, his head tilted to one side. He's waiting too. Each minute that passes is like being caught in a storm, rolling and helpless.

I answer his return call on the first ring.

"Hello?" I'm breathless. "Were you able to reach him?"

"Yes, he's at his office. I assumed you didn't want him to know about your inquiry so I just double-checked that our next meeting was still moving ahead as planned."

Tears well up in my eyes. He's safe. The horrific images of his bloodied body finally dissolve in my mind and I can finally breathe. He's not hurt. Or dead. He's just ignoring my calls.

"T-Thank you so much for doing that, I appreciate it," I hope he can't hear the wavering emotion in my voice.

"Anaïs? Would you mind if I came to visit you? Just to see how you're doing. I know you must be going through a lot, you could probably use a friend."

I'm taken aback. Just as I start to respond, the doorbell rings. Jumping up, I run down the hall.

"Um, sure. You don't have to…" I'm distracted and in a hurry to end this call.

"Great, I'll come by tomorrow in the early afternoon. Bye!"

"Bye," I rush to open the door, tossing the phone on the sofa as I run by it.

My eyes land on the flowers first, orange-colored blossoms that look soft and light. When I look up at the delivery man, a shocked gasp gets Oksana's attention from the kitchen.

"Are you alright?" She calls, coming to join me.

"Clint? What are you doing here?" I stare at him.

"I only have a few minutes. I'm here because Zion sent me," he hands me the flowers and fruit. "He can't come but he wanted me to bring these up to you. The sooner the better." He pulls a hard, round tube out of the bag on his back.

Taking it, I look up at him, waiting for further instruction. I don't even know what this thing is.

"Look inside of it," he smiles.

Turning it around in my hands, I see the end has a cap that looks like it comes open. Peering inside, I can see a paper rolled up inside.

"We should go over to the table," he points inside.

"Right, sorry, come in."

"Clint West," he holds his large, tattooed hand out to Oksana.

"Oksana Petrova," a shy smile spreads across her face.

Watching the two of them, I almost forget about the mystery tube. What is happening? Oksana shy? Never! Is she blushing?

"You are—" his tongue swipes over his bottom lip, "the prettiest damn thing I have ever seen."

She giggles and the pink tint on her cheeks deepens.

I clear my throat, I should give them a moment. Turning away, I walk to the table and turn the tube upside down. A large piece of paper slides out onto the table. When I unroll it a painful sob cracks my chest.

"What is it?" I hear Oksana behind me, rushing toward me.

"I don't know. I was instructed to bring it, so I did."

Mercy Field. The blueprint in front of me is more spectacular than anything I could have dreamed up.

"He's building this?" I choke out between sobs.

"I don't know," Clint shrugs lightly.

"What is it?" Oksana's voice is soft.

"It's just...an idea that I had. I can't believe he's doing it." I stare down at the beautiful design. The pool and the gardens look exactly like what I described to him.

"Why isn't he answering my calls?" I whisper more to myself than them.

"You've tried calling him?" Clint looks surprised.

"Yes, since last night. He's not taking my calls."

He sighs and looks at his watch. "I have to go before I get caught up here. I'll figure out what's going on."

CHAPTER 10

 naïs

THE USUAL EXCITEMENT I feel when the doorbell rings is notably absent as I walk toward the front door. The large bouquet of flowers from this morning, sweeping vines of bleeding hearts, catch my eye. An appropriate flower choice if there ever was one. My steps are slow and heavy toward the door.

I meant to decline his offer for a friendly visit but I was distracted.

Pulling open the door I'm surprised by his appearance. He looks...different. When we met he was wearing a suit that reminded me of a lemon. Now, he's wearing... a T-shirt and dark shorts.

A big smile spreads over his face when he sees me.

Maybe it's being born and raised in The Underworld but his super friendly attitude and cheerful demeanor make me uncomfortable. He doesn't know me, why is he so happy to see me?

"You're a vision," he grabs my hands. "Sunlight agrees with you!"

While I won't deny the sun-kissed glow on my skin is something I enjoy, his compliment makes me feel weird.

He's not Kane. That's the problem.

Kane would have growled, "you look fucking stunning," and my insides would have gone all gooey. Kane probably would have done a lot of things... dirty, sweaty, wet things that make me want to melt.

Jiji barks defensively as he steps into the house. He snaps and growls, his little tail standing defensively.

Gideon looks at him the same way I look at the rats in the gutter at home, disdain mixed with a bit of fear.

"Oh. You have a dog," grim annoyance is clear in his statement.

"This is Jinx." I bend down to pick up my angry puppy. "He takes a while to warm up to new people."

That's not actually true, Jinx doesn't usually behave this way, he really likes people. Red flags.

"Would you like to go on a walk? We can go down to the beach?" He suggests, looking toward the water through the windows.

I don't want to walk on the beach with him, I want to walk on the beach with Kane. The alternative is sitting here in the house with him. At least on the beach, there will be things to distract us from just... being together.

"A walk sounds nice," I try to make my voice sound convincing.

The sand is warm under my feet as we walk just above the surf.

"How are you adjusting to life up top?" He runs his hand through his blonde hair, making it look disheveled.

"I'm adjusting. It's different."

Everything here glows, the sunshine making it warm and

beautiful. It's so clean, green things grow, flowers bloom, and the breeze is soft and clear. When the unending sky slips up and allows a cloud to cut through the perfect blue, even the cloud is exquisite, white, and billowing. The sunrises and sunsets are pink and purple streaks the sky. The stars look close enough to touch, shining against a perfect black backdrop.

Why am I so unhappy here?

The Underworld is the opposite equivalent in every way, mirrored like negative exposure.

Kane and Gideon are the perfect personification of these polar opposites. Kane's dark hair and stoic attitude oppose Gideon's bright blonde and lightheartedness.

We pass a large group of people gathered in the sand. Some of them are spread out on towels, soaking up the sun, others are throwing a ball around, chasing one another.

"Oh, my God!" A girl stops mid-stride. "Mr. Cross?" Her enthusiastic squeal catches the attention of the rest of the group.

Chaotic excitement surrounds us as everyone runs over, all talking at once.

"I'm so sorry about this," he squeezes my shoulder before taking time to talk to everyone, most of them asking me to take pictures for them.

The scantily clad girls in bikinis hug into his side and press kisses into his cheek while I capture the moments on their phones for them. I feel like I'm watching this unfold from somewhere else. I'm here, I'm taking the pictures, trying to smile but my heart is a million miles away.

Why isn't he answering my calls? He's building my place, the blueprints are perfect. Why is he still building it? I hope it means that he doesn't hate me... but I left... and he's ignoring my attempts to reach out to him.

"Excuse me?" A girl waves her hand in my face, "Can I have my phone back?"

"Oh," I feel my cheeks heat, "of course, sorry."

"It's so embarrassing being recognized in public like that," Gideon puts his arm around my shoulder as we begin to walk again. I hate the way his arm feels against me. It's heavy, like it's pressing into my body.

After twenty minutes of walking, with short pauses to smile or shake the hands of excited passers-by, I have learned all of the important things about Gideon.

His favorite things. His crazy exes. And his deep and profound love for his kingdom and the people that live here.

He's very open and talkative. I don't have to drag anything out of him; he gives it all up freely. In fact, I haven't been able to get a word in edge-wise to ask a question.

"I really hope you'll be happy here. After everything you've been through, you really deserve it," He moves his arm, finally, taking it from my shoulders and letting it hang beside him.

"I hope you know that I'm here for you. What Kane did... it was absolutely disgusting. Please, don't let that hold you back. Don't let it make you mistrusting."

"I won't," I promise, thought

"I hope we didn't scare you too much. It truly was a misunderstanding."

Smiling, I nod, not sure what to say.

"In hindsight, I can see how you thought you were being kidnapped. Marvin should have been more careful with you," he chuckles.

"I thought Cohen Farly was taking me," I admit.

"I'm sure that was terrifying. Men like Farly are the lowest of the low."

I watch his face as he talks, the intensity of his emotion. He certainly seems to dislike Farly as much as Kane does. Maybe they aren't working together.

"Who is Marvin?"

"My cousin, he has the-" he gestures over his cheek. The guy with the naked woman tattooed on his face is the ruler of the free world's cousin?

We walk in silence, finally a peaceful moment to think without.

His fingers keep grazing over mine.

My mind wanders to the way Kane's hand feels in mine. His hands are so big... they're rough but somehow soft. Everything about him is powerful, his hands are no exception. He uses them without a second thought to pull a trigger, but with me... with me, he's so soft. The gentle way he holds me, how his fingers run over my skin. A shiver runs down my spine at the thought. If I close my eyes, I can feel it.

"So? Would that interest you?" Gideon taps my arm.

"I'm sorry what?" I was so wrapped in Kane's arms, that I forgot I was here, up top, on the beach... with Gideon.

"Would you like to go to dinner with me? I would love to take you out."

CHAPTER 11

ane

HANDING the unopened files back to Declan, I sigh, "Death, all of them."

The slowly healing bruises around his eyes are creased with unspoken concern. I ignore it. I don't have to explain shit to him.

The truth is, my vision is so blurry from lack of sleep I don't think I can focus my eyes enough to read the files. If I had read the files, most of them probably deserved the punishment they've been given. In the end, none of it matters.

Leaning back in my chair, I swing my legs up onto the desk. My eyelids feel like lead weights. I'm almost unconcerned enough to keep my eyes closed when I hear feet shuffle against the floor.

With great effort, I peek one eye open. Declan is still standing there, holding the files, staring at me.

"You can go," I growl and snap my eyes closed.

"Um, Sir?"

"What?"

"Zion is here, he says it's important."

Pulling myself to sit upright, I feel like an eighty-year-old man. I'll blame it on the bruises and swelling from our sparring session.

"Let him in," I sigh. If he tries to hit me again, I'm going to shoot him.

"Kane," as soon as he comes into the room, I know he's here for serious business. "I have surveillance footage that you should see." He sets a laptop on the desk in front of me and clicks a video.

"These two cars crossed into the underworld half an hour ago," he points out two SUV's on the grainy video.

"Ok." I wait.

"Watch the video at the Tartarus Road intersection, it's clearer," he clicks another video, "look at the driver of the first one."

The SUV approaches the camera and stops at the red light. The driver of the first car rolls his window down to flick a cigarette into the street. A tattoo is clearly visible on his cheek.

"I'll zoom in." Zion presses a few keys, the still frame growing larger.

"A naked woman." Now he has my attention.

"Where are they now?"

He clicks yet another video, "They parked twenty minutes ago in the underground garage next across from Hanzos, but I've watched all the footage over and over from every camera... they never leave."

Groaning, I pull myself up to my feet.

"I want every entrance and exit covered. Call everyone. We need heavy artillery, just in case. Get a team on the roof at Hanzos, snipers. That's where I want you, Zion."

His mouth pulls into a line. He's going to fight me on this as soon as he has the chance. He won't want to be separated.

"I'll cut all the street cameras on the way there, if they have tapped into the feed, they won't be able to see our movements." His voice is curt, annoyed. I don't care.

Walking toward the elevator, I feel the familiar spike in my blood pressure. It's not much, just a little punch of adrenaline before a fight. Nothing like the promise of a good blood bath to put a little pep in your step.

When the door slides open, the bartender is inside. He looks surprised to see us, then angry. Why does this guy keep popping up?

"Is it done?" Zion asks him.

"Yes." He nods.

I don't have the energy to care.

As the elevator brings us down, I can feel his eyes on me. Reaching out I grab him by the color, slamming his body into the mirrored walls with a loud crack. The glass splinters behind him.

"What the fuck are you looking at?"

His chest pushes forward, rage in his eyes, "Why aren't you answering her calls?"

My spine stiffens. "She hasn't called. I would never ignore her calls." I know he means Anais. There isn't anyone else.

"She's been calling you! She told me. She was fucking crying, man." He looks uncomfortable.

A million thoughts crush my skull all at once. Why is she calling? Is she alright? Does she need something? Does she miss me? My phone never rang..not once. How the fuck does he know she's been calling? He said she was crying.

"When did you see her?" I press him into the mirror again.

"I sent him early this morning," Zion interjects from behind us.

"And why the fuck did you do that?" I don't release his collar from my grip or turn to look at my brother. I have him pulled up slightly, standing on his toes so we are eye to eye. He doesn't blink or cower. He's brave, I'll give him that. Fucking stupid, but brave.

The doors slide open but no one moves.

"Zion," I growl. I'm fucking furious and his silence is not helping.

"I sent the plans for Mercy Fields, I thought she should see them."

Dropping his clothes I turn angrily toward my nosy, good-for-nothing, meddlesome little brother.

"Why haven't I shot you? I keep giving you chances and you keep fucking pissing me off..."

"Sir," the bartender speaks behind me.

Looking back over my shoulder, I wait, impatient for him to speak.

"She's been trying to call you since last night."

She was trying to call before she knew. That knowledge makes my chest tight.

"Was she alright? Is she in trouble or—"

"She seemed fine."

I grab Zion's shoulder, squeezing it as hard as my hand will allow, "this isn't fucking over."

As everyone slides into the waiting car, I step to the side. I feel like a child, nervous, as I wait while the line rings. My throat gets dryer with each ring.

She doesn't answer.

The glass and plastic creak in my grip. It's probably for the best that she didn't answer. Hearing her voice would have cooled the simmering rage in my blood. It's better this way...

Sliding into the seat, I nod to Declan. Time to have a little chat with our tattooed friend.

CHAPTER 12

ane

"WHY ARE YOU HELPING?" My eyes look over the bartender suspiciously. He felt he owed Anais one, that's why he warned us before but now...

"Farly is my cousin," he shrugs.

Zion's lips tilt up, whatever fucked up reason this man has for going against his own family, my brother appreciates it. He continues tapping and typing on his computer, shutting down the eyes in the city.

"Your cousin that does little to ease my mind," I raise my brows, waiting for him to explain.

"He's my cousin, but he's a son of a bitch. He fucked my wife. I have no loyalty to him. In fact, I want him to go down, and when he does, I want him to know that I was part of it." The rage shakes in his voice.

Perfect. Revenge is a wonderful motivator. I didn't trust him before but he's growing on me. No one does something simply out of the goodness of their heart. He has skin in the game, now it all makes sense.

"We have no intel pointing to Farly being involved in today's situation. Why are you here now?"

"I was here to tell Zion I completed the job. If you guys are going to fuck some people up, I'm more than happy to come along and lend my assistance. Maybe then, when it's my cousin's turn, you will allow me the pleasure of accompanying you to that… situation, as well." He adjusts the rings on his hand.

Tuning to my brother, he nods, already expecting my questions. Apparently, he checks out, the background information and history are squared away.

"What crime did you commit?"

This question causes him to tense. More than ever before, his emotions shine through anger, hurt, fury.

"I was sent here for assault with a deadly weapon and threats of physical harm. I didn't fucking do it though. My uncle… Senator Cohen Farly senior, stepped in when he heard what happened. He didn't want his son's misdeeds to reflect poorly on him during an election year. I told him I wouldn't be silent about it… I was arrested on trumped-up charges the next fucking morning."

Sounds about right. Shakespeare said it best, "Hell is empty, all the devils are here." He might not have been completely accurate, while The Underworld certainly isn't empty, all you have to do is spit and you hit a scumbag up top. For all of their moral superiority, they sure are a bunch of crooks.

"Consider today your job interview."

A smile, wicked and angry, spreads over his face. He must be hanging around my brother too much.

Declan turns us toward Hanzos. The streets are all one way over here, narrow roads with danger lurking behind every over-filled dumpster and in each shadowy alleyway.

"Stop a few blocks short. There are too many dead-end streets down there." This is feeling like a trap.

His eyes meet mine in the mirror, and he nods.

The car pulls into an open-ended alley, which gives us both advantages and disadvantages. We can get in and out of the car under cover, but if we're followed back, we'll be stuck.

"Push the dumpster out into the street. If we have to back out of here in a hurry, we want it to be clear."

Everyone nods, moving to clear the alley for our quick departure.

"My four best shooters go up to the rooftops of the surrounding buildings, facing every exit. Anyone that comes out of that garage is getting taken out." I look at my brother who nods but his jaw ticks.

"I'll go up onto the roof of Hanzos. It's the highest vantage point. I might be able to tell you where they are," Zion growls, slipping his earpiece in.

We break into groups, splitting apart to move into position around the garage. It's not a large structure. There are only five levels, including the rooftop.

It's eerily quiet. Most people are at home, sleeping off hangovers or highs from last night. At this time of day, the streets are usually mostly deserted. Something feels off, though. Call it instinct. With a twinge in my gut and my head on a swivel, we press forward.

Declan stands behind me as we inch toward one of the three garage entrances. So far, no movement or sound from anywhere.

"Yo, shit looks suspicious as fuck." Zion's voice comes through the earpiece.

"What does that mean, exactly?" Details would be helpful right now, little brother.

"Every space on the rooftop is taken, all black range rovers. There is no movement or people that I can see but—"

"That's odd."

"Exactly," he agrees.

"Everyone sound off, position one is set." I start.

"Position two, set." Each group calls out their position and status.

"Entrance teams, go," I step forward with Dec right on my heels. From my position, I can see one of the other groups silently making their way in across the garage. The bartender and another guard drop down to the ground, inspecting something that I can't see from my position.

"The first floor is empty, not a single car," he makes the outside teams aware of what we're seeing.

Shit. We're basically sitting ducks here. There are several large concrete pillars but that's it as far as cover. We move slowly, using the pillars, leapfrogging, covering each other until we're all at the base of the ramp.

Declan and I press our backs together, walking up the ramp. The second floor is as empty as the first.

Signaling the rest of the crew, everyone comes up the ramp, fanning out. This level has two ramps. We split, moving toward the ramps in two groups. There are only three more levels. The sense of calm I always feel before it's time for a fight washes over me. I take a breath, the pain I've felt over the last week is lifted.

My finger itches on the trigger. I'm ready for this.

"Fuck!" someone yells just before the ground shakes and an explosion rocks the building. Heat and ruble spray across the ground before a thick cloud of gray dust and dirt fills the air. I crouch down, Declan behind me, both of us covering our heads.

"Tripwire," the choking voice of a guard comes through.

The explosion was small, only a distraction. Standing, I press forward just as groups of men in tactical gear run down the third-level ramp in formation. Ducking behind the closest pillar, I wait to see what they are going to do.

"Twelve rows of three," I call out to my men. "We're already outnumbered."

As Dec and I move forward he taps my shoulder, pointing to an unassembled explosive device halfway attached to one of the cement pillars in the garage.

"I think we caught them by surprise. They weren't expecting us to be here so soon," he whispers and points to another device on a different pillar.

They were going to lure us here and attack. Too bad for them, my brother always has one eye on the street cameras.

"Zion, switch places with the bartender." I'm still fucking furious, but he might have saved us today.

"Fuck yeah!" He growls.

The bartender makes eye contact with me from his position, the dusty air between us settling. He brings his fingers up in a quick saluting gesture before turning and creeping toward the ramp.

"We're on the second floor," I tell Zion.

"On my way, brother! Let's fuck shit up!"

CHAPTER 13

ane

"KANE?" my earpiece fell out in the blast but I can faintly hear Zion calling my name.

Everything is chaos and confusion. The ringing in my ears makes it nearly impossible to focus on anything. Declan grabs my shoulder, helping me to my feet as we stumble through the mounds of rubble.

I'm trying to make out the damage, while still watching for the person that I can't see, who can obviously see me.

A shadowy figure moves in the distance and I shoot until it drops to the ground. Declan starts to shoot at something too, I can't see what but the sound of a body hitting the ground follows.

"He told me you would put up a fight. After babysitting the girl, I'm ready for some fucking action!" The man yells, manic laughter filling the air.

The girl? He must be talking about Anaïs.

A laugh slips past my lips. "I believe you're the man I came to see!"

"I believe that I am," he says, walking out where I can finally see him. This is definitely the man I came to see.

He looks smug. He thinks he has me.

"I'm not telling you how to do your job, but…" I can't help the smile on my face. "You should kill me right now. Shoot me. If you don't, you'll regret it."

"Where is the fun in that?" He crouches down, picking up some of the broken rocks from the ground.

"Listen, I get it. You want to play for a while, make me feel some pain… it won't end well for you, though."

The air has cleared enough that I can see the damage a bit better. It looks like they rigged the second floor to blow, reducing the center of the level to broken rock. The rest of the structure is mostly intact, though.

"How long have you been planning this?" He looks surprised by my question.

"A while. We didn't expect you to show up this early, though. We didn't even have to lure you here, so thanks for that!"

A man steps out and tries to grab Dec. He's disarmed and on the ground by our feet in less than a minute. He makes the take-down look easy despite being injured.

"I hope you brought better guys than that," my voice reflects my irritation, "otherwise you're wasting my time."

"Don't worry, we learned from the last time," he looks past me to Declan, "you killed a few of our guys. I'm glad to see you here. We have something special in store for you as well."

"Are you planning to use a Pro-Tec bridge?" Declan asks and for the first time all week, a real laugh bursts through my chest.

Tattoo-face looks confused, "What?"

"Is that how you plan to get all of the Range Rovers down… you blew up the second level? How do you plan to get all the cars down? Do you have a pro-tec bridge?"

"Yes..." he scratches his neck, "what the fuck is wrong with you? I'm going to fucking torture you! Who gives a flying fuck about the cars?" The veins in his neck bulge.

"Did you expect us to drop to our knees and beg for our lives?" I step toward him. "No. You will be doing that before days end. I told you, kill me now or deal with the consequences later."

Dec grunts behind me, falling to his knees before I have time to turn to look. One of the men behind him tazed him, the crackling spark of the electrical current still sizzling in the air.

I brace myself. The buzzing snap of the taser strikes the skin of my neck and my knees buckle. I'm not sure how many of them are on me but it feels excessive. What are they expecting me to do against ten men?

"Good night," one of the men smiles as he yanks me up by my collar. He spins my gun in his hand, gripping the barrel. I know what's coming as he brings it down against my head. Darkness creeps into my vision and her face flashes in my mind.

"Anaïs ..." I groan, my eyes fluttering open.

Well, fuck.

Declan moans beside me, or at least I think it's Declan. He's beaten beyond the point of recognition, a dripping oozing mass of blood and torn flesh strapped to the chair beside me.

"Look who's awake!"

I look past his tattooed cheek and golden smile to the man behind him.

A rough laugh bursts through my chest.

"You have got to be fucking shitting me! Cohen fucking Farly! Do you never learn your lesson?"

Farly is glaring at me from his seated position behind an entourage of heavily armed men. I can't help but notice the cast around his leg and the crutches beside him.

"How's the leg healing?" I goad him.

The blob beside me makes a wheezing sound that I can only assume is an attempt at a laugh.

Struggling to his feet with the support of his crutches, he stands but keeps his distance. The fact that he is surrounded by guards, I am tied down and beaten to a pulp and he's still afraid? A tiny ping of joy cuts through the misery in my mind.

"You're not going to think things are quite so funny in a minute..." he snarls angrily. His face is red and sweaty, his body shaking.

"We'll see," I shrug. Declan is half dead, and he's still laughing.

It takes less than ten minutes for the situation to become significantly less comical. Each guard has taken a whack at me. An assembly line-style ass whopping where my hands are tied behind my back.

I feel alive. My skin burns, and the strange tingly pressure that comes from flesh as it swells is overwhelming. I can barely see due to the injuries and blood covering my eyes. The shots to my torso definitely did some damage to my ribs but I'm peaceful. For the first time since she left, the outside and the inside match.

This situation is bleak, full of pain and violence. It feels right. Missing her so much I can't breathe? I don't know how to deal with that. Getting repeatedly punched about the face and body? That's a cakewalk. This is a situation I know how to control.

"This is Pricilla," he shows me a long-bladed dagger with an ivory handle.

"She's a beauty," I cough, watching the man with the tattoo on his face.

I'm trying to figure out exactly what is happening now. Is he a gun for hire? Is he the official connection between Farly and Gideon? Did Gideon have a hand in setting this up? I wouldn't be surprised. That motherfucker has been a few steps ahead of me at every turn.

"Maybe I'll use Pricilla to kill you with, Farly," I turn to him, and smile, blood dripping from my lips.

"Just fucking kill him!" he yells, clearly fed up with my imperturbable attitude.

"I really wanted to do this slowly, to take my time and watch you suffer but..." he brings his tattooed cheek down right in front of my face. The blade presses into the skin just above the waistband of my pants. "I guess we can have a bit of fun first."

The blade cuts through like jello. He looks over my shoulder and giggles, "clean through!"

Grunting as he pulls the blade back, I watch as blood pours from the hole he created.

In a flash of chaos and sizzle in the air, I am sprayed across the face with blood and tissue. His body drops dead on the ground in front of me.

"What the fuck just happened?" Farly screams behind him.

"Zion," I smile, forcing myself to stand with the chair still tied to my hands.

The clap of gunfire has everyone running. The group of armed men shoot into the air at nothing. They can't see where they're being attacked from. Screaming, running, the whiz of bullets, absolute pandemonium.

I knock my body into Declan's chair, pushing him over onto the ground while splintering the wood enough to free one of my arms.

Pulling myself to my feet, my breath catches. Fuck, that stab wound hurts. I snatch a gun from the clutches of one of the bodies on the floor. Through the haze, the screams, and the carnage, I see him. He's struggling toward the ramp.

"Farly!" I yell out. I've let this carry on long enough. This ends, right now.

Panic is all over him, in his erratic movements. He swings his body between the crutches, moving as quickly as he can.

"You can't outrun me!" It hurts to laugh but I can't stop it. He's trying so hard.

Dropping one crutch, he pulls a gun from his waistband. We stand still, chaos swirling around us.

My lip twitches as I raise the gun. Blood gushes from my side, the slight movement causing pain to radiate through my body. With both of our guns aimed and ready, I squeeze the trigger. My body lurches back, hot, acidic pain burning in my shoulder.

His body hits the ground just before mine does. Fuck.

My vision turns white. *"Baby,"* her soft, lilting voice echoes in my mind as I drift into unconsciousness.

CHAPTER 14

 naïs

"I'm ready," Oksana yells from the hallway.

Pulling my suitcase from my room, I fix my disheveled clothes. "Me too."

"Let's get the fuck out of here!" She cheers.

We scramble down the stairs, our suitcases loudly banging on each step, the wall, the banister, we don't care. There isn't time to be careful.

After Gideon asked me to join him for dinner, I politely declined. I tried to let him down easily with acceptable and completely non-offensive excuses.

-I'm not ready to date.

-You seem like a wonderful man, I'm just not looking for a relationship.

-It's not fair to you to have to put all my broken pieces back together.

It's like he couldn't hear me...or wouldn't. Every reasonable excuse was met with a solution that involved us together. By the time we walked back to the house, he was being almost aggressive, demanding more than asking.

"We'll go to La Vache, it's a Michelin-star restaurant, I know the chef. You'll love it. I have a lot going on this week, but I'll come pick you up, maybe two weeks from today... I have to check with my secretary."

I was so uncomfortable. Kane is demanding, he's possessive and obviously controlling but not creepy. After circling around the same conversation for close to twenty minutes, he just decided to stop asking and tell me when he was picking me up.

As soon as I closed the door behind him, I ran to Oksana's room and burst through the door. The last thing I wanted to do was force her to leave, but I needed to get out.

As she starts the engine, her face gets serious, and she grabs my hand. "Listen, I need to tell you something. When you asked if I could drive, I wasn't technically lying but... I haven't had a license in three years. I haven't driven a car since I was sent to The Underworld."

"So if we get pulled over." I cringe.

"That would be bad... also," she looks down nervously, "when we get to the border, we're probably going to be arrested. I'm not sure what's going to happen when we try to get in with no papers or identification..."

We sit, staring at each other in silence.

"Fuck it," I whisper, "let's go."

"Hell yeah!" She pumps her fist in the air. The car lurches backward and then forward as she slams on the brake. "Shit, sorry. I just have to get used to the pedals. No worries!"

My grip on Jiji gets a little bit tighter as she pulls the car onto the road.

"Is it weird that I can't wait to get back?" It's like she's reading my mind.

"Not at all."

"It's so beautiful up here, and I do miss it sometimes, but it's weird, The Underworld has become my home. I'm more comfortable there than I ever was up here." There is a sadness on her face that hurts my heart.

"I know what you mean, sort of. This place never was my home but I understand. For all of its dirty heathenism, The Underworld isn't so bad. At least everyone is bad right out in the open. No one is pretending to be something good when they aren't." My mind drifts to Gideon. He hasn't actually done anything truly bad, he just makes me uneasy.

"Ready to get arrested?" She giggles as the car accelerates.

"Hopefully Kane will come bail us out."

"Girl, I hope Clint West comes to bail us out. That is one fine piece of tattooed muscle!" She wiggles her brows.

"I knew it! You were blushing when he took your hand!"

"He's so handsome. In a gritty, tattoos and scars kind of way." Her eyes look glossy like she's picturing him in her mind. "What? Why are you smirking?"

My expression gave me away.

"Oh nothing." I bite back a smile.

"No! Don't give me that! Why are you smirking?"

"You just have a type. That's all." Zion and Clint—tattooed, muscular, bad boy types.

Her eyebrows knit together into a scowl and a telltale pink blush sweeps across her cheeks.

"I'm not judging you! Aside from the tattoos and choice of hairstyle, Kane and Zion look almost identical. Clint is also very attractive, if you're into that sort of guy." I bite my lip to hold back a laugh.

"*That* sort of guy? The super hot sort? Yeah," she snorts, "I'm really, really into that sort of guy!"

The drive feels longer than I remember. I'm so nervous. The anticipation of waiting to see him is the worst part. Joking with Oksana helps, but the lingering feeling in my stomach won't go away. He hasn't answered a single phone call or text. What if he doesn't want me to come back?

My phone is burning a hole in my pocket.

Casually, I pull it out and set it on my lap, drumming my fingers over the screen.

"You could try to call him," her voice gives her smile away.

Clearly, I wasn't as casual as I tried to be.

"It might help for him to know we're coming." I pick up the phone and dial.

The call drops before it even rings.

"Don't worry, girl. I'm sure there is a logical explanation. He's crazy for you. There is no way he would ignore your calls."

Unless he hates me for leaving.

Deep down, I know she's right. He might have lied but me not about everything. Doubts creep in, but in my heart I know, he wouldn't ignore me on purpose or without reason.

My foot taps nervously as landmarks that I recognize start to appear in the distance.

I miss the feeling of his arms around me. When I finally see him, I'm going to hug him tight. We'll have to talk and figure everything out but first thing, I want to hold him and to feel him holding me.

As we enter the tunnel, the energy in the car changes. We're both buzzing nervously. Home is just out of reach. Also, slightly concerning, we're probably getting arrested.

My skin crawls as the slow crawl of traffic has us stopped behind an incoming bus. People are screaming, their cries echoing through the tunnel, vibrating the windows.

"And to think we're coming here willingly," Oksana chuckles nervously, obviously uncomfortable.

"Is it always like this? I've never waited in this line before. When Kane and I went up top before…it wasn't like this."

She bites into her lip and looks down at her hands. "Kane did that."

"Did what?"

"He had traffic stalled so that you didn't have to hear it," she smiles. "Declan told me."

I'm ready to throw the door open and make a run for it. If I have to wait much longer to see him, I'm going to spontaneously combust.

A border guard finally steps toward us.

"Ready?" She whispers as she lowers the window.

"Ready."

"Where are you ladies headed today?" He looks confused.

"Um... well... Can you call Kane or Zion? Tell them that Anaïs is here."

He snorts and bends down to lean against the car. "I'm going to need identification and the registration information for this car."

"So, about that," she squeaks, "we don't have those things. For your own good, you should call Zion, seriously."

He runs his fingers over his mustache, "Step out of the vehicle with your hands in the air."

CHAPTER 15

 naïs

"You're really going to regret this," Oksana snarls defiantly as she is pushed roughly forward into a holding cell. The plastic zip ties they bound us with are cutting into my skin. Any humor in the situation disappeared as soon as we arrived at the small holding area. The guards have been unnecessarily aggressive, pushing us and slamming us into things. We've been compliant from the start.

The area around her eye is starting to swell where she was pushed into a wall during the pat-down portion of this horror show.

"Sure we will," the guards laugh. "Another stupid little bitch who thinks The Underworld is a place to come party."

A smile spreads across her lips as she plops down on the splintered wooden bench beside me. "You should really call Zion."

"We'll get right on that," he rolls his eyes.

I'm not sure how much time has passed, but I can see through the tiny window that the sky has grown dark. My fingers are numb, and my wrists hurt so badly that I have to actively hold back tears.

"I can't hold it much longer, Anias," the distress on her face matches my own. She's been frantically tapping her toes for almost thirty minutes. Shifting on the little bench, she tries to relieve the desperate pressure.

"My wrists hurt so bad I can't feel my fingers anymore," I wince, moving my arms for the hundredth time, searching for any position that eases the pain.

She leans back and looks behind me, "shit, the skin is broken, you're bleeding a little bit."

Jumping to her feet, she leans against the metal bars, "Hey! We need help! One of you better get down here!"

No one has come the last several times she's called out, so I'm surprised when a guard steps in front of the cell. This is a different guard than the ones from earlier.

"Listen, I'm not trying to name-drop or pull strings here but this is Anaïs Poulain," she nods her head toward me.

His eyes go wide and he takes a nervous step back, as if even standing near me was frightening.

"I see you've heard of her," Oksana sighs, relieved. "This is all a misunderstanding. Her wrists are hurt. I'm about to burst if I don't get to a bathroom and we really, really need you to make a call for us."

If he's registering anything she is saying, it doesn't show. He looks completely shut down, with glossy eyes and a far faraway stare.

"Call Zion," I stand from the bench, "He'll be easier for you to talk to. Call him and tell him where we are. I'll make sure Kane knows you did."

Sweat is already gathering on his forehead. He's panicking. It's written on his face.

"Jensen?" I read the name on his uniform. "I promise to tell Kane that you helped us. He will be pleased to hear it."

He nods his head and runs down the long hallway.

"Wait!" Oksana screams, "please! I need the bathroom!"

The loud thud of a metal door slamming closed leaves us alone again.

"Fuck!" she wiggles her body around, tears pooling in her lashes.

"Come here, you'll have to angle yourself, but I'll try to open it," I turn my back to her, moving my aching hands.

"Your hands are turning blue." She moves the button of her jeans around my senseless fingers. We move, twisting and turning, fumbling around until her button pops open.

Just as the zipper slides down, the door creaks open. Jensen has scissors in one hand as he shakily unlocks the cell door.

"I called the security chief, who left a message with Zion. I'm waiting to hear back from him." He cuts the zip ties, and I can't help but cry out from both relief and pain.

"Fuck," he whispers to himself as he turns to cut Oksana's ties.

"Bathroom, where?" She's already running down the hallway before he answers.

"The door before you reach the stairs!" He yells after her. "Y-You're really going to tell Mr. Azrael that I helped you right? I just started my shift. I wasn't even here when you were brought in." His eyes are pleading and full of fear.

"I promise, I'll tell him."

His phone rings in his pocket, and he pulls it out quickly, fumbling it in his hands.

"Hello? - yes, sir - yes - Anaïs Poulain, sir - she's right here." He hands me the phone.

"Hello?"

"Anaïs? What the fuck is going on?" It's Zion and he sounds —weird.

"Zion, what's wrong?" The hairs on the back of my neck stand up as his ragged breaths come through the phone.

"We got caught up in some shit today. I'll be there in five minutes, sit tight. Are you alright?" I can hear his footsteps clicking against the ground.

"We're fine. I'll see you in a minute." I want to ask about Kane but he's already hung up.

Poor Jensen is so nervous he drops the phone as soon as I hand it back to him.

"Holy fuck, I've never had to go so bad in my whole life!" Oksana rejoins us in the narrow hallway.

"Zion's on his way," as I say the words Jensen drops his phone again, the screen shattering against the concrete floor.

"Jensen, it's going to be alright," I try to help him relax, but he starts pacing back and forth. His anxiety is only adding to his nervousness. All my emotions from early on have come back with a vengeance. Zion is coming to get us. I will be face-to-face with Kane before long.

After several minutes, he seems to pull himself together enough to stop pacing but he still looks terrified.

"Let's go wait in the employee break room," Jensen's voice is thick with tension. "I'll bandage your wrist."

We follow him down the hall and up the stairs. A few men are inside the dingy break room with flickering fluorescent lights.

"Jensen, what the fuck are you doing?" One guard from earlier jumps up as we enter. He steps forward and reaches out to grab me. Oksana pulls me back while lunging forward, putting herself between us.

"Back up! Don't grab at her like that. She's hurt because of your fucking cuffs!" She snaps at him, blocking him from me.

Everything happens so fast. The guard pushes her back, her body colliding with mine as we're both pressed into the wall.

His hand locks around her throat, and he brings his face so close to hers their noses are touching.

"Who the fuck do you think you are?" He screams, his hand raises above them, poised to hit her. "You stupid fucking–"

A tattooed arm reaches in, grabbing him roughly by the collar and jerking him away. The guard is slammed into the wall, his face against the exposed bricks.

Zion. The smile on his face fills me with terror, even if he's not directing it at me.

"Finish that sentence," his voice is calm, soft even. It doesn't match his expression at all.

"Z-Zion, sir. This prisoner was–" he fumbles.

"Let's hear it. What were you about to say to her?" He's unfazed by the man's obvious fear.

"Cunt. I was going to call her a cunt." His voice shakes. The other guards cower back.

A visible shiver runs through the man as Zion starts to laugh. He's unhinged. Loud, happy-sounding laughter fills the room.

"Thank you for that," Zion brings a finger up to wipe a tear from below his eye. "I have had a terrible day. It's just been one thing after another. You know how it is..."

The guard looks so confused.

A heavy sigh pushes past Zion's lips, and for the first time, I look at his clothes. He's covered in blood.

"I don't have time to do this properly and frankly, I'm too tired, so this will have to do." My eyes pinch closed as he pulls a gun from his waistband. I feel a hand on my wrist, pulling me forward. With my eyes still closed, I let myself be led away.

The deafening pop of gunfire makes my body shutter. An overwhelming sense of dread squeezes my stomach.

"Let's get the fuck out of here," Zion joins us.

My eyes flutter open and I'm met with his blood-spattered face.

"Zion, you don't seem injured." A wave of nausea washes over me.

If it's not his blood...

He gives me a curt nod and continues toward the door.

"It's his blood, isn't it?" That's the only thing that makes sense. It's obviously not Zion's blood. Kane's not here. He would have come if Zion had called him, which he would have done if...

My heart nearly stops.

"He's hurt, Anaïs. It's bad."

CHAPTER 16

*A*naïs

I'M JUMPING from the car before Zion even stops. As fast as my feet can carry me, I'm through the parking garage and to the elevator bay. I can't hear anything beyond the pounding of my blood in my ears.

When he said the word gunshot, everything else faded away. He's been shot. Someone shot him. I tried to listen to the rest of what he said, but I couldn't focus. All that matters at this moment is getting to him. I need to see him with my own eyes.

When the elevator doors open, the bloody mess inside makes my stomach roll. Looking down, I notice the drips and smears across the floor of the garage, too.

Sweat trickles down my neck and my hands shake. I have to get to him now. In a frenzy, I press the button in the elevator only to have it remain open.

"Fucking close! Goddammit!" I scream as I pound my fists against the wall.

Zion and Oksana step inside but I can't stop myself. Any control or composure I once had has disappeared into a hysterical panic. Everyone, even Jiji is looking at me like I'm deranged.

"Wait!" The thought suddenly hits me, "why aren't we at the hospital? Why is he here if he's been shot?"

Zion sighs and rubs his hands over his face. For the first time since he picked us up, I really look at him. He is utterly exhausted. Under the blood, I can see the toll that today has taken on him.

"He won't go. The doctor is up there, his wounds are through and through. Doc doesn't think he needs surgery but... the blood loss is concerning. He just won't go in..."

Like hell. We're going. Now.

As the door slides open, I run, following the trail of blood on the floor toward his bedroom.

"Kane Azrael!" I don't even recognize my voice. Rage. I'm so angry at him. I'm mad that he's hurt, that he's being stubborn, that he's in pain. Mostly I'm mad at myself. How could I not be here?

When I reach the room, he's lying on the ground. A doctor is trying to connect his arm to a line of blood but he's moving and mumbling. I can hear him saying my name. I'm not sure if he heard me or if he's just calling out. Either way, my heart cracks open.

"We're going to the hospital. Right.fucking.now!" I drop to my knees beside him. The sight of his bloody broken body extinguishes my fury in an instant.

"Baby," he smiles up at me weakly, his one good eye meeting mine. When his bloody hand comes up and touches my cheek, he draws in a sharp, pained breath. "You're really here? Is she really here?" He turns to the doctor.

"Yes, I'm here. We have to go to the hospital, Kane, please. You've lost too much blood." I take his hand in mine, holding it to my chest.

"Ok," he nods.

"Jesus fucking Christ," the doctor growls, "Is that all it takes for you to get him to see reason?"

Congealed blood oozes from large cuts on his forehead and across the bridge of his nose; one side of his face is swollen and purple. A bandage wraps around his bare chest and stretches up over one shoulder. Another bandage around his stomach has blood seeping through it.

His hand goes limp in mine and his eyes flutter.

"Kane?" I shake his uninjured shoulder, but he doesn't stir. "What's happening? Why isn't he opening his eyes?"

"We need to get him to the hospital right now." The doctor looks nervous.

Zion rushes over, pulling him up over his shoulder, "Let's go, hurry the fuck up," he grits, struggling under Kane's weight.

The elevator, the car ride, it's all a blur. Oksana holds my hand, tethering me to the ground as a group of doctors and hospital staff load Kane onto a gurney and wheel him away.

When he finally disappears from sight, I crumple to the ground. My wobbly knees simply give out.

"He's going to die. He's going to die and I've been up top, taking time. Why did I need time? I love him! He loves me... he didn't want me to leave him. Is that such a terrible thing? Did I really need space because he lied to keep us together? What if he dies?" I'm breathless from my frantic rant.

"He won't die." Zion's voice is steadfast.

"You don't know that! He-"

"Anaïs, he won't die." I look up at his face, searching for doubt. There is none. He's steady, completely sure.

Hours pass as I pace the hall, my tears never ceasing. Oksana is sitting with Zion, her legs hanging over his lap. Everyone is exhausted, but there is no sleep. I cannot close my eyes. I can't sit down. If I sit down, it's like the weight of the world crushes me. Grinding down on my shoulders. I have to stay moving; it's the only thing keeping me sane.

The double doors at the end of the hallway swing open and a man in blue scrubs approaches us. My heart is in my throat.

We rush toward him, surrounding him as he pulls a scrub cap from his head.

"He's going to be down for a few days, he needs to let his body rest and heal. We gave him four units of blood over the last five hours. The wound in his shoulder should heal with no adverse effects, the bullet passed clean through and managed to miss all bones and tendons. The stab wound to his abdomen gave us a bit of trouble. It missed his organs, but we had to close up a few pretty severe bleeders."

"Can we see him?" The desperation is clear in my voice.

"One person at a time can visit with him until he wakes," he nods.

"Oh," my chest falls, "you should be there, Zion. He's your brother..."

His deep chuckle makes my heart hurt. He sounds so much like Kane. "Go, Anaïs. If he was awake and able to choose, he would not pick me."

CHAPTER 17

 ane

WAKING up is like being dragged down to hell by my ankles. It doesn't matter how much I fight against consciousness comes. The dreams were so vivid, so real. I could feel her skin. She was all around me, holding me, whispering in my ear.

My skin burns, a deep radiating heat in my stomach and shoulder. I was stabbed and shot...the memories tickle in like dripping water. The puzzle slowly putting itself together. My face hurts more than anything.

Forcing my eyes open, I realize one eye is too swollen for me to see out of. What the fuck, I'm in the hospital? I remember being absolutely clear about not being brought here.

Wait...

She was there. I thought I was hallucinating, but she was actually there, I remember. That's why I'm here. She swore at me.

A slight movement beside me makes my heart stop.

She's here. Curled in the bed beside me. It dawns on me that I must be dead. I died, and this is some kind of afterlife vision. An apparition. I hardly breathe, not because of the pain but because I don't want to move. I don't want to somehow make her disappear.

This feels different from the dreams that have tormented me. The physical pain is grounding. I think this is real.

Fuck. My chest tightens painfully, and my lungs burn. My rapid breaths are suffocating. I can't get enough air. Monitors start to beep loudly in the room.

What the fuck is happening?

I rip at the needle in my arm, pulling it out. I need to get out of here. Ignoring the way my body protests to my movement, I sit up in the bed.

"Kane!" Anaïs' voice cuts through my brain like a dull knife, ragged and slow, torturous. "Kane, please don't try to stand."

"Mr. Azrael," a doctor and several nurses burst into the room, "your oxygen and heart rate monitors are reading abnormally."

I rip a plastic cap from my finger and throw it across the room as I take a step away from the bed.

"You have to get back in the bed. Your body isn't ready for these kinds of movements yet," the nurses try to stop me as I drag my body toward the door. The room spins and my vision goes blurry. Is this a heart attack? I think I'm dying.

"Kane?" The hurt in her voice adds to the immobilizing panic I feel.

"Mr. Azrael, we need you to lie down." They start spouting out reasons for my inability to breathe—a blood clot or shock.

Her hands grip my arm and the chaotic screaming in my brain goes quiet, "Kane, take a breath."

It feels like my chest is being crushed by a weight. I can't inhale enough to get any air. I feel her soft fingers on my face, gently holding my cheeks.

"Breath in," she encourages me. I can see the worry creasing her face but the corners of her lips tick upward. A little smile that feels like a hammer chipping away at the boulder on my chest.

I'm sinking into quicksand. My head is so far below the surface, I'll never break free. When she leaves again, be it tomorrow or six months from now, I won't survive it. She's here because I'm hurt, then she will leave again.

Jerking out of the comfort of her touch, I let my body fall back into the bed.

It takes every bit of the strength in my body to close my eyes. I want to look at her face, to touch her body, but I can't.

The ache in my chest is more painful than the wounds scattered over my body.

The nurses flutter around me, reattaching wires and monitors, and checking my pulse, temperature, and oxygen levels. I sit still for about fifteen seconds, letting them run around. They're touching me too much. Their hands on me feel like sandpaper.

"All right, enough!" My voice comes out growling.

"Just a few more things Mr-"

"I said enough! Back the fuck up!" All of them quickly step back, dropping their hands by their sides.

"Leave."

Like ducklings in a row, they almost run from the room.

"Kane?"

Her voice dives down into the abyss like a lifeline, just waiting for me to grab it so she can pull me back up to the surface. I feel the bed dip down by my feet as she sits. "Look at me, please." The confusion in her voice is clear.

My eyes land on her. She's watching me, staring at me so intently that it stirs something in my soul. I look away, down at her hands. I don't want her to see me and it helps not to make eye contact.

There are bandages around her wrists.

"What the fuck are those?"

"Oh, um," she's hesitating, "let's not worry about that right now. What just happened? Please, let the doctor look at you-"

An angry sound rumbles in my chest, "What are those?"

"Um, well, Oksana and I—we were arrested when we tried to come back into The Underworld."

"What the fuck!" My anger takes over and I reach forward, pulling her tiny hand toward me to inspect her injuries. "Are these from handcuffs?"

"No.."

"What then? Who fucking did it?" I see red. As I carefully remove the bandages, the extent of the damage to her perfect skin becomes visible.

"They used zip ties."

Is she being purposely obtuse? I look up and she's chewing her lip. Goddamn it. The little wrinkle in her nose is so distracting.

"What happened? Why are you trying to avoid this conversation?" My voice is noticeably softer, even to my ears.

"I want to talk about you, about what happened. I want to talk about us. This doesn't matter." She touches her wrists. "I don't care about what happened earlier; there are more important things right now." Her eyes look glassy, tears welling up before sliding down her cheeks.

"I want to know who hurt you."

"I couldn't stay up there anymore. I've been calling you over and over again. You weren't answering, and I thought…" Her voice wobbles. "I had to come home. So, we got in the car. Um, your car, we took your car. We didn't have any identification or papers, so they arrested us at the border. They wouldn't call Zion…so we sat in the cell for hours. One guard finally came down and helped us. My zip ties were too tight, that's all. I'm fine..." she rushes through so fast that she has to suck in a big breath at the end.

"I would never ignore your call."

She just stares at me, studying my face. I haven't seen myself, but I can only assume that I look similar to road kill. She's still looking at me with such care that it makes me feel restless.

"I shouldn't have gone to the beach house," she finally whispers into the blaring silence.

"You look thin."

She blinks, her head tilting to one side.

"You're mad at me." She isn't asking.

"No." I'm not mad, not at her anyway.

"Then why are you being like this? I mean, is it the drugs? Should we wait to talk? You're... why are you so far away from me? Why do you keep flinching when I touch you? Why are you acting like I'm some stranger? I've called you... please tell me what you want me to do or say to make you stop looking at me like that!" Tears roll down her cheeks, dripping down her chin.

Reaching out, I take her hand in mine, pulling her into me. My shoulder burns as I let my arms circle around her. The feeling of her skin touching mine is like a crack in glass. It starts small, but it grows, the split spreading until the glass breaks. Light peaks in through the fractures, illuminating the darkness enough for me to see all the horrible, ugly things that grow in the depths of me.

She will leave again.

CHAPTER 18

 naïs

IT DOESN'T SEEM to matter how I phrase it, the answer is always the same.

What's wrong? Are you alright? Is something bothering you?

I'm met with a curt and emotionally void "I'm fine."

I don't want to annoy him. I don't want to nag. I can feel there's something wrong. It's like an itch on my skin that won't go away. He's not fine. *We* aren't fine. I just don't know what to do.

Whatever it is it feels like an invisible barrier between us. Even when he's beside me, I feel like I can't touch him. Physically, I can reach out and take his hand, I can feel his skin but it's not the same. I can't feel his heart like I used to.

I've been home for a week and things are awful. I've started showering twice a day so that I can sob without him hearing me. It's the only way I can manage to keep it together.

He doesn't hold me; he doesn't kiss me. He hardly looks at me. I want to rip my hair out and scream. He's so withdrawn that he won't even stay home with me. He went in to do judgments today, broken body and all. I didn't ask to go because I felt like it would bother him.

The thought of being annoying to him makes my heart hurt so bad I can't catch my breath. My dad made me feel like that, like I was irksome and my presence was irritating. Kane never made me feel like that.

I don't know what I was expecting when I came back but this is not it. There has been no discussion, not on anything. The sinking feeling that he doesn't want me here is starting to grow with each passing day.

The elevator dings and I jump up. Zion walks in and my chest deflates. I'm suddenly hit with unexplainable anger. Seeing Zion makes my hand itch. I think I want to punch him.

"Hey, I wanted to talk to you," he steps toward me.

"Yeah, likewise..."

"You go first," he sits down.

"Why did you come up there on his behalf, telling me about how miserable he is? He doesn't seem like he was miserable at all. In fact, I'm starting to think that you were lying to me and he was doing just fine while I was gone!"

"Whoa!" He stands up and takes a few steps away from me, "Are you going to swing at me?"

I hadn't realized that my fists are balled up by my sides.

"No," I drop my face into my hands. "I'm sorry, Zion–"

"What's going on, Anaïs?" His tone is more serious than I've ever heard it.

"He won't talk to me, or touch me... it's like... it's like he doesn't remember me or something. I don't know what to do." I press my nails into my palm, trying to distract myself from the burning lump in my throat.

"What the fuck? That explains so much... he's still stomping

85

around, sending everyone at judgment to death without even opening the files. Did you have a fight?"

"He's sending everyone to death without even looking at the crimes?"

"Yeah, shit has been tense. He shot at his secondary driver yesterday." He says so casually that I'm sure I heard him wrong.

"What do you mean, he shot his secondary driver?"

"No, not shot, *shot at*," he says, like that makes it better. "Luckily, his shoulder is still fucked up, so he missed."

"Zion, What do I do?"

"I came here hoping you had the answer. Fuck–" he stops as the elevator opens.

Kane steps out, his eyes narrowing at us before he walks past us to the bedroom.

"I'm going to go before he finally makes good on his threat to shoot me," we nod at each other before quickly moving in opposite directions.

He only walked by a moment ago but by the time I make it to the bedroom, he's already in the shower. Taking a deep breath, I pull my shirt over my head. Stripping out of the rest of my clothes I take quiet, tiptoeing steps. I'm so nervous as my feet touch the cool tile floor.

With the way things have been going, I'm afraid he might reject me.

He's standing in the shower, the silhouette of his figure visible through the frosted glass.

"Kane?" My voice is quiet but by the way his shoulders tense, I know he heard me.

Reaching out my hand, I run the tips of my fingers over his wet skin. A deep, low moan fills the shower. The steam is thick and warm and it feels heavy in my lungs. Grabbing his arm, I pull slightly, hoping that he will turn around.

He turns, his eyes are wild as he racks them down my body. I can feel it physically. It's been so long since he put his hands on me that this is almost more than I can bear.

With trembling hands, I slip my fingers lower. The muscles in his stomach clench under my touch.

"What are you doing?" The roughness of his voice sends a shiver down my spine. There is no warmth or softness in it. I'm no different from a person in judgments. He hates me.

"I need you, Kane, please." My voice cracks.

Pulling me forward, he spins and pins me to the wall. My face presses into the cool tile. I can feel him behind me, so close, but not close enough to touch me.

My body reacts to his nearness, calling out to him. My mind is reeling, though.

"You want me to fuck you?" He rubs himself against my ass, hard.

"I want you." a whimper crawls up my throat.

His hands slide down my stomach, pressing flat against my skin. Goosebumps spread over my body. I can feel his breath on my neck, his wet skin against mine.

Spinning so that my back is to the tile, I look up at him.

"I want you," I whisper again, my voice thick with the emotions that burn in my throat. I want him to understand. Physically, yes, I want him. I need more than that, I need him the way I had him before. I want his heart.

Craning my neck, I try to catch his eyes but he won't look at me.

Pressing myself against him, I bring my hands down between us. When I wrap my fingers around him his chest rumbles.

"Kiss me," I feel like I'm begging him.

CHAPTER 19

 naïs

INSTEAD OF KISSING ME, he bends to slide his hands under my thighs, picking me up. Without a word, he walks out of the shower.

Setting me on the counter, he adjusts himself between my legs.

I feel him, pressed heavily against my entrance. My body wants this so bad, I'm practically drooling but I also feel like I might burst into tears at any moment. I've been longing for his touch. Now that I have it, everything is wrong.

He's touching me, nearly sliding himself inside of me, but he's not here. He won't look at me. His touch is only sexual, he won't put his hands on my face or slide them over my neck. The soft kisses he usually peppers all over my skin are gone. This is like sex with a stranger. The tenderness I usually feel, the softness in his eyes, the attentiveness, it's gone and I miss it.

I miss him and he's right in front of me.

A strained grunt, then a low relieved sound, heaves from his chest as he slides himself into me fully.

Somehow in such a short amount of time, I forgot how full he makes me feel. Our bodies are laced together in the most intimate way. He's pressed deep inside of me but I feel empty. There is no passion or spark, this feels meaningless.

Reaching up, I grab his face in my hands, trying to force him to meet my eyes. If I can only make him see me. If I can make him feel the connection that we normally share.

His eyes are pinched shut. The muscles in his chest are so tight that they shake under his skin.

"Kane, look at me!" I press my mouth to his chest, to the healing wound on his shoulder, to his chin. When I reach his lips he moans against my mouth. I move my hands to his shoulders, holding myself to him, anchoring myself down.

With each thrust of his hips, the tightness in my stomach grows, winding into a ball.

"Fuck," he groans, pressing himself deeper.

"Oh, God," I'm overwhelmed. I feel myself getting closer, but my heart hurts so bad tears drip down my face. He looks like he's in pain, too. Each time our hips connect, he groans a deep, wounded sound.

Despite the sadness, the pleasure is too much to ignore. He's closed off and detached, but it's still Kane. I can't help the way my body reacts to him.

My body tightens around him, pain and pleasure bursting through me.

When he stills, twitching deep between my legs, his eyes flash open. His grip on my hips is so tight on my hips that it's painful. When our eyes meet, a choked sob rips from deep in his chest. For a brief moment, everything fades. His eyes are locked on mine and he's my Kane again.

I pull him forward, slamming my mouth to his. My whole body hums as he moves his lips against mine. A fluttering feeling starts in my heart and sweeps through me, bubbles under my skin. His hands move, circling around my waist to pick me up into his arms.

Just as hope blooms in my chest, everything comes crashing down. He rips himself away from me, setting me down on my feet and storming out of the bathroom.

"Stay with me, please," a broken sob cracks my chest. I can't avoid this for one more second. Following him out into the bedroom every emotion feels like it's crashing down on me, pummeling me into the ground.

"What just happened? You were there, I saw you! I could feel you!"

"Nothing happened, Anaïs," he sighs, agitated.

"Something happened! What is wrong?"

"Nothing, come to bed." He angrily adjusts his pillow before lying down.

"Stop saying nothing! It's not nothing, it's everything. Where is your heart, Kane? Why won't you talk to me? Why won't you look at me?" I'm sobbing openly.

He angrily rolls out of the bed and walks toward the closet. I can hear things rustling around before he comes out with sweatpants on.

"I'll be back," his voice is monotone. The same way it's been since I arrived here.

I block the doorway, standing in his way. "Be honest with me! This distance is ripping me apart! If you don't want me anymore, you have to tell me if you want me to leave... please, just talk to me." I choke.

He brushes past me. "There isn't anything to talk about, Anaïs. How many times do I have to tell you? Just leave it alone."

I stand, watching him pull his shirt on as he leaves me standing in the doorway. I'm frozen, looking out into the dark hallway waiting for him to turn around. When the elevator dings, I turn, running toward the closet.

My heart pounds in my chest as I pull a small bag from one of the shelves, stuffing whatever I can find into it.

If he doesn't want me here. I won't stay.

I took one week to think about how we could move forward in our relationship after his mistakes. That's all it took for him to call it quits.

Through my anger and the ache in my heart, a small voice nags in the back of my mind. Something is wrong. He lied, yes, but I know his heart. Dropping the bag onto the floor, I pull a shirt on and crawl into the empty bed.

Lying alone in the dark, I force the tears away. If he won't talk to me, I'll have to figure out another way to get him to open up. I'll fight for us, for him, even if he seems unwilling.

ane

I CAME BACK an hour ago and found her curled in the middle of the bed. A bag of her things is packed on the floor in the closet. The broken sound of her voice and the tears on her cheeks play over and over in my mind.

I can't sleep. She's been here for seven days and I still feel like she's slipping through my fingers like sand.

She's beside me in the bed, her body beside mine. We might as well be miles apart.

I know why she left, why she needed space. I lied to her. I tried to control her. The rational part of my brain understands why she would need to reconsider whether or not I was worth continuing with. What I don't understand, the part that keeps me awake, is why she came back?

I'm caught in an inescapable circle. Missing her was worse than any other pain, physical or otherwise, that I've ever endured, but at least I understood that. She was gone. I ruined it, that's that. Now she's back.

Every part of me is sure she will leave again. I will fuck this up again, it's inevitable.

As long as I don't get too comfortable, I might be able to survive her unavoidable departure from my life.

Don't get too comfortable with her hair on my pillow while she sleeps.

Don't get too comfortable with the way she reaches for my hand to hold.

Don't get too comfortable with the little kisses she likes to press to the corners of my mouth.

This uneasy, skeptical feeling that knots in my stomach just at the thought tells me that I am a fool. It doesn't matter how prepared I am, when she goes, the darkness she leaves behind will consume me.

I'm holding myself back from her, building a wall between us. I was blindsided by the depth of my feelings for her. Now I live, perpetually on the edge, waiting for her to walk away again. It's been a week and the heaviness is crushing me, grinding me into dust. Not touching her, not kissing her, it's my own personal hell. I know once I give in I won't be able to stop.

She wants honesty. She wants things from me I don't know how to give. Being honest and open? I'm not even sure I can learn that. What I know are the things that would crush her, my tiny flower growing in the mud.

With all the love I feel for her, I still hurt her. I'm sure I will again. I can't let myself be the reason she withers away. To save her, I have to sacrifice myself. When she leaves again, I have to just let her go, completely. I'm bracing for it, like waiting in slow motion for imminent impact.

She stirs, rolling over in the bed, the sheets tangle between her legs.

"What's wrong, Kane?" she whispers, her hand gliding up my

stomach to rest on my chest, just over my heart. She scoots her body tightly into mine, pressing us together.

"Nothing, go back to sleep."

"Kane," she hesitates, "please, talk to me." I feel her lips grazing over my pulse, kissing my neck so softly. She's not going to let this go. She's going to ask every day until I say something more than nothing.

"Anaïs, there isn't anything to talk about. Sleep." My voice is too harsh. I don't mean for it to be, but it is rough and angry. There is only rage inside. Rage that ruins and destroys.

"Something is wrong. I can feel it. Why have you been killing everyone that comes to judgment without even looking at the files? Why? Why don't you hold me the way you did before?" Her breath shutters. Fuck, she's crying again.

I'm going to find out who told her about the judgments and throw them from my fucking roof.

I bet it was Zion. That's why he was here tonight. To snitch on me.

Holding her tighter to me, I try to ignore the gaping black hole in my chest. She feels it, too. The rotten, oozing darkness is spreading from me to her.

"Are you... did you..." she stutters, a quiet whimper spilling past her lips. "Did you want me to stay away?"

I didn't, but she should have. I don't know how to tell her that I know this is going to end badly. How do I explain that being without her, I am only an empty shell, and I'm preparing myself for when I return to that miserable state?

She's broken my whole life down and rearranged it into something that I never knew existed.

I'm crippled with the fear of losing her, of hurting her. I can't be the reason she hurts, the cause of her pain.

"Please," her plea breaks through the turmoil boiling at the base of my skull. "Tell me what to do. Tell me how to help you."

"You can't."

Promise never to leave me? I can't ask that. When I fuck it all up, she will have to go to save herself.

She sits up, her knees touching my chest. Her tear-stained face looking down at me, studying me.

"I can if you let me. Tell me what's making you so sad."

Sad? Is it sadness? I think it's rage and darkness.

"Will you trust me? Just tell me, don't pull away, whatever it is, no matter how bad or ugly, just tell me..." The burning trail her fingers leave over my skin makes it hard to think.

Trust her? Trusting her will be the thing that ends me. This tiny woman, with all of her soft edges, will be the thing that tears me to shreds. She holds me in the palm of her hand, a worthless speck of dust that she could and probably should throw away.

I cut my bleeding heart out and gave it to her. At every moment, it feels like she's going to take a blade to it, ripping it open, twisting and tearing it apart.

Trust her? I don't even trust myself.

With a sigh, I sit too, moving so that no parts of her are touching any parts of me.

How can I explain this? Everything is lodged in my throat, the words and emotions, the fear. It's lumped there, choking me.

"I love you so fucking much it hurts when I breathe."

Her breath hitches, but she waits.

"I want you here with me, but I don't understand why you came back. I hurt you, and I know I'll fuck up again. When you leave the next time... it will ruin me. It cut the legs out from under me. I don't think I'll be able to do it again."

"I came back because you apologized, Kane. I believe you when you say that you're sorry you lied." Her voice is so sweet and sincere.

"Why? Why would you believe that?"

She blinks, thinking, "Because that's what you do when you love someone Kane, you trust them."

"But what if I hurt you again?"

"That's the thing about trust, baby," she scoots closer, her knees touching my thigh, "I'm handing you the power to hurt me because I love you. The risk is worth the reward."

The risk is worth the reward. Those are terms I understand.

CHAPTER 21

*A*naïs

CRAWLING UP ONTO HIS LAP, I hold his face in my hands. The stoic, simmering anger is gone. His eyes meet mine with the same soft sweetness I'm used to.

"It's scary, isn't it?" I whisper as I graze my lips over his. "Giving someone the power to destroy you."

He takes a shuddering breath and I can smell the faint scent of whiskey.

"I was miserable without you," I give him a deep, wet kiss before pulling his bottom lip into my mouth. "I missed you every second. I thought of you all day and dreamt of you all night. We have to talk about our expectations for truth and honesty in this relationship, but right now... right now I just need you."

His need for me is pressed, hard, between my legs. It makes me lightheaded just thinking about all of the things I want to do to him.

He rolls suddenly, pinning my body beneath his on the mattress.

"You aren't going to be able to walk for a week," he growls before gripping the neckline of my shirt. The fabric rips down the middle like paper.

A breathless gasp escapes my lips as he licks and kisses his way down my body. When he reaches the tops of my thighs, he sits back on his heels.

"Open." He uses his hands to pry my legs apart.

He looks unhinged. His eyes flit back and forth over my body looking at my face and the now aching spot between my wide-open legs.

Sliding down onto his stomach, he presses his face between my legs and inhales.

"Kane," I can feel my cheeks heating.

He ignores me, leaning in to take another deep breath between my legs. With his flattened tongue, he licks a strip from the bottom to the top. Each stroke of his tongue is deep, lapping and slurping like he's eating ice cream.

"Oh, my *god!*" I press my hand to my mouth, biting into my palm to quiet the loud unstoppable sounds I'm making.

His hand comes up, pulling my arm down. "Those sounds belong to me and I want to hear them." His voice is stern before he goes back to his tormenting.

Loud moans, panting breaths, and sighs fill the room until I can't take it anymore. With his hair tightly in my grip, I call his name into the early dawn haze. He swipes his thumb across his chin and lower lip, wiping away the wetness from his face.

Sitting up, I press my hand to his shoulder as he tries to crawl over me. "Sit down," my voice is raspy. "Take off your pants and sit up by the headboard."

His mouth twitches, but he complies.

"Yes, ma'am."

Biting into my lip, I watch him, his broad shoulders pressed against the headboard with his long legs stretched out over the bed.

When I let my gaze fall from his face, lower and lower...my body clenches. He's holding himself, his large hand moving slowly up and down. The emptiness between my legs aches and flutters.

Crawling forward, I grip his arm, stopping his movements. It's ridiculous and embarrassing, but I'm jealous of his hand. I want all of his pleasure. I want my body to be his only means of climax.

I'm taking control. Tonight, I want to say all of the things I usually hold back. I want to whisper the same dirty words in his ear that he does in mine. I want him to whine and beg, to need me so desperately that he can't think straight. The way I need him.

"I want to make you feel good."

He groans and lets his head fall back as I bend forward on my knees. Slowly, I let my tongue slide from his balls up to his thick-capped tip.

He sits up straighter, the muscles in his stomach trembling. I make the same motion again, pressing my tongue harder.

No words, just sounds, raw, scratchy sounds in his chest and throat propel me further. Stretching my mouth around him, I watch his hand grip the sheets.

"Fuck-" his voice falters as I take him all the way to the back of my throat and hum. I'll never fit all of him in my mouth, but I can make sure what fits feels good.

I move like this, taking him deep, vibrating around him, then sliding up and down. A pattern that has his whole body twitching. Whenever he gets close, I back off. Over and over again.

"P-Please," his tortured begging makes me drip between my legs. "Baby, please ride my cock." He barely gets the words out.

In my selfish need to feel him, I let him slide out of my mouth. His thick, swollen head falls down onto his stomach.

Crawling over his body to straddle his hips, we're face to face. His lips graze my cheek, his panting breath fanning my cheek.

"I've missed you so much." My emotions get the better of me as he runs his hands over my thighs. Having him so close yet so far away has been the worst kind of punishment.

Sliding down, I take him in with one fluid motion. He groans and rolls his hips up.

"No," I press my hands to his chest. "I want to make you come tonight." Lifting my hips, I drop them down, rolling at the end.

"Fuck," he growls, and his hands squeeze my hips.

My body burns with need. I want him more, harder, deeper, faster. It feels like nothing can satisfy this awful aching tightness in my stomach.

His blown-out gaze is focused on his cock, watching it fill me again and again, while I drip all over it. Leaning forward, I suck the skin on his neck, over his chest and shoulders.

"Are you giving me hickies?" He lets out a strange half chuckle mixed with a moan.

Slamming my mouth to his, I pour everything into him. I want him to know, to feel it without any doubt.

"Anaïs," his voice is raw, broken. "I won't ever lie to you again." He promises, his breath fanning over my neck.

"I love you," I feel my body starting to tighten, the unraveling feeling ripping me apart from the inside out. I'm heavy and weightless as his name rips from my throat.

His face is pressed into my shoulder. "Baby," he growls softly as he twitches inside of me.

A tangle of limbs and sweaty skin sliding together, he pulls me into his chest. We're nestled down under the sheets, our bodies pressed together so that as much skin is touching as possible. His arm is wrapped around my shoulders his fingers in my hair.

"I thought if I held you at a distance, it might hurt less when you leave." His chin rests on the top of my head.

"What happens if I never leave?"

"I'm going to fuck up again. I don't know how to do this. Being happy—love— it's-"

"Terrifying," I finish his sentence. "You probably will *'fuck up'* again." My voice dips over the expletives.

A tired laugh bursts from his throat.

"I'll make mistakes too, Kane. People fight, and sometimes, we will anger each other. That doesn't mean I'm going to leave." I run my fingers over the round scar on his shoulder.

At some point, our voices fade, consciousness slipping away as the sun comes up.

CHAPTER 22

ane

"IS THE BLINDFOLD REALLY NECESSARY?" Her nose scrunches up.

"Yes."

My driver keeps looking at Anaïs in the mirror. When we make eye contact, he glances toward the road again. I should have waited until tomorrow when Declan is back to do this. I just can't wait anymore.

The thought of showing her the site for Mercy Fields has my stomach twisting and fluttering. Every time my mind wanders, I notice my knee bouncing anxiously. What the fuck is wrong with me?

Last night, after we loved each other until she couldn't keep her eyes open for another second, I looked it up.

-Fidgeting, sweating, muscle spasms, restlessness. Apparently, those are all signs of nervousness or anxiety.

I'm not nervous. I just want her to see the progress that's been made on her place. I want to make sure she likes it.

The fluttering feeling is burnt to a crisp by the fiery anger that radiates from my spine when I catch the driver looking at her again. What is he looking at? She's fucking gorgeous. But she's mine.

"When I shot at you last week, my shoulder injury prevented me from hitting you. I'm feeling much better today. Keep your fucking eyes on the fucking road, or I'll pluck them out, and then shoot you. This time, I won't miss." I growl, and the car swerves slightly.

"Y-Yes, Sir. I'm sorry, sir."

"Kane," her soft hand reaches for mine, feeling down my arm until she reaches my fingers.

She probably won't be pleased if I shoot this kid. Taking a deep breath, I lean into her, letting the smell of her hair lull me into a state of quiet calm. The car follows the road out of the concrete jungle and into the vast wasteland of rocky, barren nothingness.

The car stops beside the fleet of construction vehicles parked on the dead-end road. The hilly land has been leveled into large slat platforms, where different buildings and gardens will go. Further in the distance, more land is being flattened where houses will be built.

The trucks are loud, rumbling and beeping, heavy loads of dirt being shifted from one place to another. I watch her face for a moment before removing the blindfold. She's trying to piece together what she's hearing, but I'm not sure she has a frame of reference. It must just sound loud and chaotic.

Several workers are leaning on the back of pickup trucks, drinking coffee and water. When they see me, they clammer to find their helmets and rush off to work.

Her fingers tighten around my hand as she takes cautious steps.

"I'm not going to let you fall," I whisper against the shell of her ear.

Leading her to the end of the road, just before the asphalt ends, I stop her. Slipping the blindfold down, she blinks, adjusting to the light.

"What is this?" She's awestruck as she steps forward. "Is this…" her delicate voice trails off.

"Obviously," I clear my throat, "there is still a lot of work to be done but…"

"It's perfect. Can I go in there?" She gestures to the dirt.

Searching a few of the trucks, I find a hardhat in one of the beds. After placing it on her head, we walk forward into the dirt. She looks so cute.

With her hand in mine, we stomp through the dirt making our way through the different sections.

"This will be the garden?" She points to the vast expanse in front of us.

She must have really studied the blueprints if she knows the layout with no markers or visual clues.

"Yes, and the greenhouse will be over there."

"It was one thing to see the blueprints but to be here…in person…wow," her voice is breathless.

"Mr. Azrael," Tom, the foreman, approaches warily. He's probably nervous to see me here. Our previous interactions were not particularly pleasant.

"Tom," I gesture to her. "The boss is here now. Anything that still needs to be finalized goes through her."

The worried crease between his eyes softens some when he looks at her.

"It's nice to meet you, I'm Tom Buchanan," he extends his hand.

"Anaïs Poulain," she smiles, "what you've done so far is truly incredible." Her eyes roam over the piles of dirt and rock like its something extraordinary.

I walk a few steps behind them, watching her as they make plans. She's confident but sweet, asking and never demanding.

Tom is at ease. Their discussion is easy and open, both of them bouncing ideas off of one another, expanding on the other's suggestions.

I don't ask; I demand. I dictate and expect results, if not instantly, down to the minute of time it takes to complete the task.

People fear me, they do it for me out of fear. They respond to her, they do it for her because they want her happy, because they like her.

Declan, Oksana, the bartender... even my brother. They want her to be happy for the sake of her happiness. There is no other motive, like self-preservation, needed.

The thought makes my chest feel warm. My sweet angel. I'm not the only one that is enchanted by her.

"I was wondering, would it be possible to make some kind of body of water that isn't a pool? Something that looks like a lake?" She asks and I step forward, waiting to ensure that he responds appropriately.

"That is possible, but we would have to dig out more land. There isn't room for something like that in the current boundaries. There is also the issue of water access. The only water we have is the Styx, and that is not water anyone would want to swim in unless they were actively trying to grow a third eyeball. We could use the mountain up top and create pipelines that bring the glacial water down, but that would be incredibly costly-"

"Whatever she wants, she gets."

He turns to me wide-eyed.

"Anything she wants," I reiterate

He nods and turns back to her. "There are some incredible man-made lakes up top. I will get you some pictures and we can go from there."

After Anaïs pours over samples of everything from cobblestones to street lamps, we're in the car. Today went just as I had hoped it would, but now, I'm ready to get her home alone.

"Thank you so much, Kane," she scoots her body toward mine. "I can't believe it's actually real, that it's going to be a real place..."

When I press a kiss into her hair, she tilts her head back, bringing her mouth to mine. Soft and sweet. My phone rings, forcing us out of what I had hoped would eventually lead us to the bedroom.

"What?" I growl.

"How likely are you to kill someone right now?" Zion's voice comes through the phone.

I already don't like where this is going. "The likelihood was low until you called. What's going on?"

"I've got the analytics back on her phone."

CHAPTER 23

$\mathcal{A}$naïs

His jaw is clenched so tight I'm worried about his teeth. We hold hands as the elevator takes us slowly up to meet Zion.

He sighs deeply. "I wanted to take you to bed."

"I wanted you to take me to bed," I whisper against his chest.

A groan rumbles in his chest. "As soon as he leaves."

He takes my hand and rubs it over the front of his pants. The thick outline of his hard cock makes me shiver.

I squeeze him just as the elevator opens.

"*Fuck.*" I hear him mumble under his breath as I walk out. The thick raspiness of his voice makes me want to drag him to our room.

Zion is outside on the balcony, tugging at a chew toy with Jiji. When he sees us his playful expression darkens. My stomach is in knots. Whatever he found, it's bad.

My phone is lying on the sofa next to a stack of papers.

As soon as he opens the door, it starts to ring.

"Don't answer that," he says, pulling his mouth into a grim line.

Picking up the papers, he hands each of us a packet.

"The highlighted parts are attempts you made to call him." We look over the multiple highlighted rows.

Kane hums angrily before sitting on the sofa and pulling me into his lap.

"There is a bug on your line. You couldn't call down to The Underworld." He sighs and rubs his face. "Do either of you know how phone calls actually work?"

I don't; I look at Kane and see him nodding that he doesn't either.

"This is where it gets confusing. When you make a call the radio waves travel through the air to a cell tower." He pauses to make sure we're following. "Those waves are then sent to the tower base station where they are routed to the phone you're calling. When your calls got to the base station, they were being held, and you were being fed a fake voicemail message. The calls were never actually being made though... nothing ever came through to Kane's phone." He hands us more paper. "These are Kane's records, there are no incoming calls from your number."

My phone vibrates loudly. Kane reaches for it, but Zion snatches it away.

"It was a simple hack that made sure you couldn't call each other. The block is on your line as well," he continues. "I've removed them...the origin of the block is impossible to trace, but..."

"It was Gideon. Who else would do that?"

I can't stop my surprised gasp. "Why would Gideon do that?"

"Um, can I speak with Anaïs alone?" Zion asks.

"Why?" Kane's body tenses behind me.

"I just... there is something I want to talk to her about." Zion looks nervous.

Sweat gathers on my neck. Why is he nervous? I don't have anything to hide... what could he possibly have to say?

"Can Kane stay? Whatever it is, I'm sure he can hear."

Zion sighs and runs his hand over his face.

"Gideon has called you thirty-eight, well, I guess, forty now. Forty times today." He taps a few buttons on my phone and a voicemail starts to play.

"Anaïs, I'm knocking at your door. Is everything alright? I'm here to pick you up for our date." Gideon's voice comes through the speaker.

Kane tenses again. I can feel his eyes on the back of my head. His arms are still wrapped around me, holding me to his chest.

"I-I said no." I feel frazzled. I just got him back. I don't want this to send him into a spiral. "He asked me to dinner, and I said no. He kept asking and I was so uncomfortable. Finally, he just told me that he was coming to pick me up. That's the day we left. I... I called him and asked if he would call you. I wasn't getting through and I was afraid something happened to you. He basically invited himself over and we walked on the beach. Then, as soon as he left, we left. I was hoping he wouldn't show up... then I forgot about it completely..." I feel nervous trying to explain this. It's not exactly a believable scenario.

Kane kisses my hair and squeezes me gently. "Relax, baby. I believe you."

I let out a sigh of relief.

"If you had wanted to go on a date, I wouldn't be angry. That is your choice." His voice is strained. "I hate him, but I can't blame him for wanting to take you out."

"I didn't want to."

His chin comes to rest on my shoulder, and we look at Zion, whose mouth is hanging open.

"I thought you were going to kill me just for mentioning it. Wow. The messages get progressively worse—louder, angrier." He hands me the phone.

Clicking the last message, I am startled by the loud, angry message that starts.

"You stupid fucking bitch! You went back to him?" Gideon screams through the speaker.

Kane tenses and his arms squeeze tighter around me.

"You picked the wrong one... No one chooses him over me, not even his own father. You will regret this." When the message ends, an uneasy knot rolls around in my stomach.

Seconds pass into minutes of agonizing silence. I can feel the muscles in his chest and arms shaking as he holds me. I have so many questions, but I don't think now is the time to ask.

"Tell me you have good news on the facial recognition," he finally says. His voice is rough and furious.

Zion's shoulders slump. "The guy was a ghost. We can't connect him to Farly or Gideon anywhere on paper. We know he was involved because he kidnapped her and he stabbed you."

My head spins. "Wait, who?"

"The guy with the tattoo on his face, he was with Farly in the parking garage." Zion runs his hands through his hair.

"Martin or Marvin..." I rack my brain, trying to remember.

"What?"

"He's Gideon's cousin, he told me!"

"Cousin Martin?" Zion mumbles to himself, his brows furrowing as he thinks. "I don't remember a Martin..."

"Find someone," Kane growls, "we need one living person that we can connect to this, one witness to Gideon's connection to Farly. Search for all living relatives, obviously, there are some that we don't know."

"I'll put out a dragnet. We'll find something." Zion jumps up and starts calling someone as he walks to the elevator. He doesn't look up or say goodbye.

The door barely slides close and Kane is storming toward our room with me in his arms.

"We're in a shit storm, but all I can think about is burying myself inside of you," he groans and I clench.

Suddenly, that's all I want to do.

CHAPTER 24

 ane

I NEED HER. Right now. As I lay her down on the mattress, I feel like I'm not in control of my body. I'm running on need, on instinct, on lust and love.

Pulling her shirt over her head and ripping at her pants, I have her naked beneath me in no time.

I need to feel her, to have her skin touching mine. As I yank at my belt, her fingers move up, working to open the buttons of my shirt. Knowing that she is as desperate to feel me as I am for her makes the pressure of my cock against my pants almost unbearable.

"Fuck," I groan as I pull myself free. The relief is short-lived. I need more. I need the relief that only her body can provide.

Pressing one of my fingers into her, I rub and massage the soft, wet skin. "I'm going to fuck you so hard I want to hear your moans echo off the walls. "

She cries out, the raspy, low sound that makes my cock leak. I can't pull my eyes away from her, from the glistening skin between her legs.

"How did I get so lucky?" I haven't done much good in my life, but I must have done something right to have her. It's still a struggle to understand how *she* wants *me.*

"Kane, love me please," she whimpers and I can't wait another second. In one hard thrust, I'm as far into her as I can possibly reach, our hips pressed tightly together. Rocking back, I push into her again and again.

She's surrounding me, pulling me into her, the tight massage of her pussy making me delirious. When she wraps her legs around my waist, pulling me deeper, I push faster.

She's moaning and arching her back from the mattress. I'm panting and groaning, my body searching for release. Sliding through her, forcing my body into hers, my spine starts to tingle. The indescribable static feeling that spreads through my limbs and short-circuits my brain. She's wide open, and drenched. The wet sound, the squelch of every thrust, is my favorite sound. Maybe it's my second favorite sound, the first being the soft, raspy way she sighs my name as she comes.

"Fuck, I want to put a baby inside you." I freeze as soon as the words leave my mouth and she gasps.

"Jesus Christ," I sit back, pulling out of her completely. "I-I don't know why I just said that..."

She's still staring at me, wide-eyed, with her lips slightly parted.

"Kane," she whispers, but the blood pumping through my ears makes it almost impossible to hear her. I don't want kids. I never have. I can't raise a child. Not even a tiny, perfect miniature version of her mother.

"Kane," she reaches up and grabs my face in her hands, pulling me from space back down to solid ground.

"I—I'm sorry. I-" I'm floundering.

"Did you mean it?" She tilts her head to one side. Her face is the picture of calm. If she's panicking, she's hiding it well.

"No! I mean...fuck. I can't be a father. I've never even considered a child. I..."

A small smile spreads across her face, and she presses a kiss to the corner of my mouth. "We don't have to talk about it right now, you can take time to think but we should discuss this eventually."

Laying down beside her I try and fail to force my thoughts to anything else. Beside me, she looks completely at peace. Her eyes are closed softly and her slow, steady breaths move her chest.

"Do you want kids?" I choke on each word.

She rolls over beside me and puts one hand on my cheek. "I never really thought about it until you said that. Now I can't stop thinking about it."

The shudder in her breath makes my cock twitch. Fuck.

"I can imagine a little boy that looks like you." Her dreamy whisper feels like a hand wrapped around my throat. She's so calm. The thoughts running through my head are paralyzing, but she is perfectly still.

"Kane, this is just a conversation. I'm not pregnant. Take a breath," she kisses me, sweet and reassuring.

"I keep seeing a little girl," my voice sounds like my throat was scraped against gravel. Clearing my throat, I look into her eyes. "She's a small angel that looks just like you." My fingers find her strawberry hair running through the strands.

"I don't want you to panic but... if it was real— if I was—can you think about how that would make you feel?" She's so gentle, like I'm a wounded bird she's trying to help.

Just the thought feels like a weight on my chest but... I also feel warm. Not warm like being burnt, warm like the sun is shining on my face. I can picture her, my baby growing in her belly, holding a tiny child to her chest...

"I wouldn't even know how to... I don't remember when I even saw a child last... my own father was... why do you think Zion and I are so fucked up? I can't have a kid."

"I don't think you're fucked up. You're a leader, you're fair but stern. I've seen your love and felt the gentleness in your touch. We might need to work on patience," she smiles, "but you would be wonderful."

"Fuck."

"I'm not saying let's have one right now," she giggles.

"The thought of actually... I'm so fucking hard." My cock twitches. Unexpectedly, thinking about this is making my whole body ache for her.

Her fingers graze over my throbbing shaft, pulling a groan from deep in my chest. "We can finish this discussion later," she swings her leg over my hips, grinding her wet cunt over me, torturing me.

"Kane?" She looks down at me. "Would you... can we do it how we did at The Playground?" The blush on her cheeks and the shyness in her request makes pre-cum drip down my cock. She wants it rough?

"Face down into the mattress," I sit up behind her, holding tightly to her hips. Spreading her legs open, I stare down at her, wide open in front of me.

When I rub myself against her, she whimpers. I slide into her slowly, gripping her round ass and using it to pull her back harder. With each harsh impact of our hips, she moans, tightening around me like a vice.

"Are you about to come?" I still holding her on the edge.

"Yes, please, don't stop!" She sounds close to tears at the thought of my prolonging this.

Sliding back, I fuck her so hard her knees slide out from under her with the force. As I feel her tightening again, I reach my hand up, slapping it against her ass so hard the sound echoes in the room.

"Oh my god," she screams, and her body trembles. Her orgasm is so intense that the pulsating grip on my cock makes me come without warning.

Her body slumps forward, soft and spent. I sit back, watching my come drip out of her. "Fuck, I want to go again."

CHAPTER 25

 naïs

SOMETHING IS WRONG. As we park outside of Kane's office, there are too many cars here. I squeeze his hand and he rubs his thumb over my skin. If he's concerned he doesn't show it.

"Do you know what's happening here?"

"No." He seems calm but I can see his eyes on the door.

"Let's turn around, let's go home," I beg as he pulls me into his arms.

"Gideon," he whispers against my hair, "Gideon is here."

My whole body goes rigid. "Why?"

"I guess we'll find out." he kisses my forehead and slides out of his seat. Walking around the car he speaks to Declan quickly before coming to open my door.

The lobby looks normal. It's as if I'm expecting a monster to jump out at us. When nothing leaps from the elevator to attack us, I try to relax.

As soon as we step out at the top floor my stomach drops.

There are at least ten men here, all of them armed, standing with Gideon.

One man lunges forward, instantly screaming when he sees Kane. "You motherfucker! You killed my only son! I'll have your head for this!" Some of the men grab him and hold him back from reaching Kane.

"Senator Farly," Kane nods his head, no fear or intimidation on his face.

"Kane Azrael," another man steps forward, "You're under arrest for the murder of Cohen Farly Jr."

The room spins and I have to grab his arm to keep myself upright.

"Everything will be alright, Anaïs," he whispers in my ear before pressing a kiss to my forehead. As the man secures his hands behind his back and mirandizes him, I'm sure I'm going to faint.

"Dec, call Zion," he tells him while holding eye contact with me.

"K-Kane," I'm frantic. I can't focus on anything. A million thoughts are racing through my head all at once. Fear courses through me. Reaching forward, I grip his suit jacket in my fists, holding onto him tightly. Pinching my eyes closed, I will myself to wake up. This can't be really happening.

"Anaïs," his voice is crystal clear in the chaos of my mind. When I look up at his face, I'm surprised by how completely calm he looks. "Take a breath, baby."

The man jerks him away, yanking him backward toward the elevator.

I feel like my feet have grown roots. I'm stuck, watching in slow motion as he is pulled away from me. Why isn't he fighting back? Did he know this was going to happen? None of this makes sense. Is he being arrested for killing Farly? But he's Kane. I didn't think he could be arrested for anything!

"Wait!" I register my own voice as I'm running into the

elevator, slamming my body into his. I wrap my arms around him and hold him as tightly as I can.

An arm grabs me roughly, ripping me away from him.

"Be careful with her," Kane growls and I feel the grip loosen slightly. I'm pulled away from him and back into the lobby. The doors slide closed, and I feel like I'm going to be sick.

"Miss," Declan holds my arm, steadying me.

"W-We need to call Zion, right now," I turn to him.

"I already did, Miss."

Turning around, I'm faced with Gideon, Senator Farly, and a few men. The look on Gideon's face has me balling up my fists. He looks so smug.

"I will be taking over as ruler of The Underworld until all of this is sorted out," he has the audacity to sigh as if this isn't what he wanted all along.

"Actually, Mr. Cross," Declan speaks from behind me, "according to Mr. Azrael, Miss Poulain is his successor to the throne."

"What?" We both shout at once.

"She is the heir presumptive to the throne and his estate upon his death or in any situation where he is unable to hold the throne." Declan shrugs like what he's saying isn't absolutely insane. "She's the Queen of The Underworld. Long live the Queen." A smile pulls at his lips.

"No, absolutely not! She can't! This is absurd!"

He's not wrong... this is absurd.

The elevator slides open, and a disheveled, out-of-breath Zion bursts into the lobby with Clint right behind him.

"You mother fucking snake! I can't believe we didn't see this coming! You better sleep with one eye open, you little bitch because we're coming for you!" He charges toward Gideon who tries to look tough behind his guards, but I can tell he's afraid.

"Send me the documents where he names her as his successor. I want to have them checked by my legal team!" Gideon yells from the safety of his shielded position. The remaining men file into the elevator with him including Senator Farly who stares at Clint like he's about to kill him.

As soon as the door closes, I sit down in the middle of the floor.

"He has no idea who he's fucking with!" Zion punches his fist through the wall leaving a gaping hole near the elevator door.

"Where are they taking him?" I whisper to no one in particular.

"I'll find out, Miss." Declan tells me, crouching down beside me.

"He was so calm, Dec. Did he know this was going to happen?"

"No... I think," he hesitates, "I think he was calm for you..."

The thought that he composed himself and didn't fight back at all for me, is the drop that breaks the dam. I sob rips at my chest and I cover my face with my hands. Last night we were talking about babies... now he's been arrested on murder charges...

"Anaïs, look at me," Zion is sitting on the ground in front of me. "I found a name... one of the Marvin Cross' men. He's hiding somewhere down here. I will tear each building apart with my bare hands until I find him. We will figure out how Gideon is involved in all of this, and we will get Kane out. Until then, we need you. You're the Queen."

CHAPTER 26

 naïs

GENTLY, I lay a blanket over Oksana and Jiji. They fell asleep on the floor of the living room in the early hours of the morning after watching me pace for almost a full day.

Every detail from the moment I was snatched by Gideon's men plays over and over in my head. I feel like a stupid pawn. Gideon didn't think he was saving me. He knew exactly what he was doing. When Kane said he was trying to take him down, he was right.

He used me against Kane, hurting him and distracting him by pulling me away. I fell right into it.

I wonder if Senator Farly knows that Gideon was sending his son's men to fight Kane? Farly was just a pawn too, a piece that Gideon moved to work in his favor.

The elevator dings and my heart stops. It's never Kane, but my heart can't help but hope.

It's Clint. I hope he doesn't notice how my shoulders slump.

A nervous sheen of sweat drips down my neck. Zion, Declan, and Clint have been coming to check in every few hours, but there hasn't been any real news.

"Zion is on his way to talk to you but... I have to tell you something..." he fidgets and punches his hands together.

"OK," I wait, hardly able to breathe.

"Kane did not kill Farly. I did."

I'm not sure what to do with that information. Kane told me that he shot Farly.

"When the bombs started going off, I ran. I climbed to the roof of Hanzos and watched until I got a clear shot. They were both hurt, aiming at each other. They shot at the same time, but Kane was so badly injured his shot didn't hit. I took Farly out."

"I appreciate you telling me, but I don't think it matters. Gideon wants Kane out of the picture. The truth about who shot Farly isn't going to make a difference except that they might throw you in jail, too."

Sitting down on the edge of the sofa, I hold my head in my hands. I feel like my head is too heavy for my neck. My body hurts, the tension and stress feel like it's pressing me into the floor.

I'm the Queen? I'm not fit to be Queen! How am I meant to do this without him? I wish I could use my power to free him but Zion explained it doesn't work like that. Once charges are filed they have to receive judgment. Since his charge is brought by someone up top, his judge will be Gideon.

The elevator pings again and Zion bursts into the room.

"He's in the pits. Let's go!"

I jump up and run to our room, grabbing the first pair of shoes I see. "I'm ready!"

"I'm not sure how this is going to play out," he warns me on the ride down. "Normally, no one would try to question me but with Kane imprisoned. You're going to have to play the 'queen-card.' It might be the only way we get in."

"I'll do whatever I have to do." I nod.

"Listen," he turns to me, and the seriousness on his face makes my blood pressure spike. "I don't know what condition he is going to be in. They probably put him in a private cell, but if they didn't... You need to prepare yourself for what you're walking into. I'm sure he planned to keep you from ever setting foot there."

The car lurches out onto the road, cutting off several other cars as we speed down the street. The sun is starting to rise, and the dirty orange sky glowing around us.

The smell of the river Styx makes my stomach feel queasy. The rolling water lapping at the shore as we drive past at a dizzying speed. As soon as the large, gray building comes into sight, I feel myself shrinking down in my seat.

The Pits is an imposing mass of stone that holds misery inside. The windowless building sits like a fortress on the shores of the toxic river.

As the car stops, an overwhelming sense of dread forms a knot in my stomach. This looks like the kind of place you might enter and never walk out of. It's the kind of gray that seeps into your soul. If Kane wasn't in there right now, I would have Zion drive away as fast as the car could take us. Clint shifts nervously in the back seat, even he is uncomfortable being here.

The moment I push my door open, I hear it, I *feel* it. A buzzing, the low vibrating rumble that physically rocks the ground. When I turn to Zion his mouth is set in a grim line.

"It's the screaming. It's thousands of people screaming all at once."

Clint mumbles something under his breath and shoves his hands into his pockets. There is something very unnerving about watching a large man fidget nervously. Whatever we're about to face, it's growing larger and more imposing by the second.

I have to get Kane out of here. He's been here for almost a full day. The thought makes my empty stomach heave.

I follow him around the side of the building to a door that is built into the wall. We're immediately met with heavily armed guards in full protective gear.

"Zion," one man acknowledges him with a slight tip of his chin.

"Where is my brother?"

"We've been told that The Underworld is under new management," another man steps forward, his bulletproof vest almost rubbing against Zion's chest.

Zion smiles and takes a small step back, creating a space between them. "That is true."

"Then I suggest you leave before I throw you into a cell for breaking into The Pits." There is something antagonizing about his smile.

"Exactly who do you think you're taking orders from now?" his brow quirks upward.

"We were told Gideon Cross is ruling over everything..."

Zion laughs, the manic, unsettling laugh that only he can conjure up. "You think Gideon Cross is ruling over The Underworld?"

They look back and forth at each other nervously. The silence is excruciating. The guard's confidence is dropping by the second. The smugness in their expressions is quickly replaced with anxiety.

Clint uses his thumb to point at me.

"'Let us through or you will have the honor of participating in the queen's first solo judgment tomorrow.'"

Tomorrow? I try to keep my face from letting a reaction show.

"She's the ruler of The Underworld?" One of them says with laughter in his voice. They both look much more relaxed than they did only a second ago.

"Yes." I take a step toward them. "Tomorrow's judgment is already pretty full. Maybe, we'll put them in a cell until I have enough time to get to them, or we could just kill them now."

Their faces change quickly change. "Wait, you're serious?"

"Very. Where is Kane?"

"Miss Poulian?" I turn to see Jensen walking out of the office.

"Jensen?" We both look shocked to see each other.

"Are you here to see Mr. Azrael?"

"Yes." I practically jump out of my skin.

"I'll take you to him." He turns and starts walking down the same hallway he just came from.

As we follow him, Zion bends slightly, whispering in my ear, "You surprised the shit out of me! Long live the Queen!"

CHAPTER 27

 ane

GROANING, I spit the blood from my mouth. Fire radiates in my chest as I chuckle, the burning in my ribs making me cough painfully. I hate to admit it, but Gideon was two steps ahead of me all along.

When it comes to Anaïs, I have blinders on. I should have seen this coming. I played right into his trap.

A hand grabs me, pulling me off the wall and into the middle of another group of angry prisoners.

"How hard the mighty falls, huh, your majesty?" A snarling man smiles before kicking me in the ribs.

I've got to give it to Gideon, putting me in the pits—with the people I've sent here was genius. They are going to rip me apart slowly. I'm sure he's relishing the thought right now.

Just as a fist makes contact with my face, the sharp, shrill sound of a whistle fills the air.

"Everyone step back, get to your cells, now!" I feel an arm on mine, pulling me up from the ground. I expect to be tossed into a cell but he leads me out of the general population room and down the hall.

"Mr. Azrael, I'm putting you here, in private holding..." he ushers me into a small, quiet room. When I turn to look at him, I recognize him immediately, even through my swollen eyes.

"I'm sure you don't remember me. I'm Todd Jensen from-"

"You helped Anaïs." I cut him off. "Of course, I remember."

He looks surprised. "You spared me. I'm returning the favor, sir." I didn't expect to have an ally here.

"I'll come check on you before the end of my shift," he locks the cell door. I assume that is more for my protection than to keep me inside.

Sliding down the wall to sit on the cold brick floor, I listen to the sound of misery all around me. Sobbing, screaming, begging, retching... it bounces off the walls. Strobing lights start to flash.

Jesus Christ, Warden Davies is really a sadistic bastard. I give him free rein here to do as he wishes with prisoners... I guess his wish is torture. Maybe I should tighten his leash a bit if I ever get out of here.

Leaning my head back, I close my eyes. With her face in my mind, all the background noise fades.

Despite the blinking lights and wailing, I find myself slipping in and out of consciousness. Her face lulling me to sleep.

"Kane?" Her voice echoes in the dark, calling to me, cutting through the horror of this place.

"Kane?" She calls again as the door to my cell opens with a loud clang.

My swollen eyes search the darkness, the flashing lights illuminating the room long enough to see her, like a shadow floating across the floor. It isn't until her hands sweep across my cheek that I realize she's here and I'm not imagining it.

"Baby? What the fuck are you doing here?" I grab her into

my arms, holding her against my chest. I never wanted her to come to this place. The sounds, the smell, the suffering—she doesn't belong anywhere near a place like this.

"Your face," she whimpers, holding me in her hands, "what did they do to you?" She sniffles and presses kisses on my bloody, sweaty skin.

Zion is standing in the doorway. He should have known better than to bring her in here.

"I'm alright, it's a few punches, nothing that won't heal. You shouldn't be here-" she shuts me up by pressing her lips to mine. She's kissing me like she thought she would never see me again. There is a desperate need on her tongue as it slips between my lips.

"We're going to get you out of here, Kane. I swear it. We won't sleep… " she sobs, her fingers gripping my hair at the base of my skull.

I can barely hear her over the noise but the ache in her voice is loud and clear. It's like a spear slicing through my heart.

"You have to sleep, you have to take care of yourself."

"I can't sleep without you…not while you're in this place," her mouth is back on mine, soft and tender, needy and aching. Her thighs squeeze around my hips, her body clinging to mine. I never thought I would end up in here. I definitely never thought I would be in here hard and desperately kissing her.

"Baby, you have to get out of here." I groan. I need her to leave but I don't want her to go. Every second that she spends in this place it's like salt being rubbed in my wounds.

A sharp, pained scream filled with so much anguish it makes my heart rate accelerate. She tenses in my arms, fear in her eyes as she looks frantically around the room.

"You have to go, Anaïs."

The look on her face is worse than any possible torture they could dish out in here. Her chin wobbles and she drops down, pressing into my neck. Her fingers grip my shirt tightly, like she's trying to anchor herself to me.

"Baby," I run my hand through her hair. Closing my eyes, I force the words out, "I'll see you soon."

"I'm doing judgments tomorrow," she shifts so that her lips graze my ear. "Tell me you believe I can do it."

Fuck.

"You can. Remember, they are there for committing crimes. Think about everyone you are sparing by taking people off of the street who don't follow basic rules."

"No murder, no rape, no assault," she shudders against my chest.

"That's right." I press a kiss into her hair. "Go." The word burns acidic in my throat. Turning to Zion, I nod and he steps forward, grabbing her arm gently.

For a moment she struggles, holding onto me tightly, ripping my heart out.

"I love you. We'll get you out, I promise." A tear slides down her soft cheek.

"I know, baby. I believe you."

She stands, letting Zion lead her out of the room, that suddenly feels colder and more miserable.

"Jensen," her voice is serious, "take care of him."

"Yes, ma'am," he nods.

CHAPTER 28

 naïs

WIPING the back of my hand over my mouth, I make sure that there is no evidence of vomit left behind.

Patting water on my burning cheeks, I stare at myself in the mirror. This is it. When I walk out of this room, the weakness, the fear... it's gone. I can fall apart tonight while I wear his shirt and cry in our bed alone. Right now, it's time to be Queen.

I have to do this. Kane needs me.

Rolling my shoulders back, I force my spine straight. Taking a deep breath, I walk out of the bathroom where Declan and Zion are waiting.

They're both watching me as if they expect me to try to run away.

"Declan, listen," my voice shakes so I clear it. "If I have to sentence someone to death... I-"

He puts his hand up, stopping me. "I've got you." He nods and pulls the door open.

My heels click against the ground as I walk to the front of the room. Quiet murmurs swirl in the air. Sitting, I look immediately at the first file. Before I lose my nerve, I have to just... do it.

"Paulie Samuels."

A large man in a sweat-stained wife-beater steps forward. His greasy black hair is slicked back on his head. He smiles at me as he approaches. He's not afraid at all.

"Mr. Samuels, you're charged with aggravated assault. It says here," I look down at the file, "that you disfigured a man over a parking space?"

I wait for him to respond.

"Mr. Samuels?" I quirk my brow at him after he remains silent.

"I like to park there." He lifts his chin arrogantly.

What would Kane do? Taking a deep breath, I pull my jacket down, straightening the front.

"Death."

"Whoa! What? Who the fuck are you anyway-" His voice is cut off but the deafening pop of Declan's gun.

Assault, murder, rape. Kane does not let those things slide. I won't either. I won't allow The Underworld to fall into chaos without him. If people think that I'll be soft, that they can do whatever they want now that he's in prison, they've got another thing coming.

He believes in me. I steady my trembling hands in my lap.

"Next," I call out into the now panicked room.

Thirty judgments later, I'm mentally and emotionally exhausted. Just as I slump back in my seat, Zion busts into the room. The nauseous pit in my stomach will have to wait. Whatever he has to say, it's important.

"We found him, Anaïs. The man who came down with Martin Cross is hiding at Hanzos. I'm going right now. Once we have him, I'll come get you-"

"I'm coming with you." I jump up suddenly, full of energy. Every moment that Kane spends in that place takes a year off of my life.

As Declan drives I can't stop my body from moving, my knee bounces, my toe taps, my fingers drum. Every second that passes feels never-ending.

"Things might get ugly here. Clint is meeting us... if you need to leave, Dec will take you home."

"Zion, I appreciate your concern, but please, don't worry about me. Just do what you have to do to get the information." A smile spread over his face as I speak.

"I thought you were mousy," he laughs.

I shrug. That's not an inaccurate assessment. I can't be mousy right now, I can't cower. If I don't step up, Gideon will take control of The Underworld and Kane will never be released. I won't let my inexperience and naivety negatively impact him ever again.

Declan parks across the street from Hanzo's and we jump out quickly, on a mission.

Zion rolls his neck and pulls a gun with an extra-long barrel from his waistband. He stops mid-stride and turns to me, studying me.

"Here." He reaches into his hip holster and pulls out another smaller pistol. "That's loaded, be careful."

I pull the slide back, just as Kane taught me, loading a bullet into the chamber.

Zion chuckles and shakes his head. "I'll never underestimate you again."

After only a moment of waiting, Clint pulls up and jumps out of his car, eagerly.

"Let's do this!" He's as pumped up as Zion.

Clint and Zion stand in front of me, with Declan following closely behind. As we approach the door the guard stands and raises his hands slightly. It looks like he won't be putting up a fight.

Once we're inside, Declan locks the door behind us.

"Hanzo!" Zion yells at the top of his lungs. "We have business!"

My ears strain in the silence, listening for any sound. After a moment, there is a creak from above us, the thump of footsteps walking across the floor.

"You have five fucking seconds before I turn this place into a heap of rubble! Hurry the fuck up!" He screams again. The thumping becomes louder and each step quicker than the last.

"Zion," he steps cautiously down the stairs, his creepy brother right behind him.

"You know why I'm here."

They look nervous, more slimy with sweat than normal.

"Surely, I don't-"

"Cut the bullshit. Where the fuck is he? We want him, not you, but if you don't hand him over, I would absolutely cream my pants while torturing you until you give him up." Zion turns to Clint, who clashes a wide-eyed menacing smile.

"I'm thinking we go straight for the balls," Declan says behind me, pulling a blade from a hidden place in his belt.

"Wait, wait, that won't be necessary. He's hiding in the money cage in the basement." Hanzo crosses his hands over his stomach, covering the front of his pants nervously.

"See how easy that was?" Zion brushes past him toward the door. "Open it," he gestures to the metal door.

With slow steps, he walks toward the door and enters a code into the keypad.

"Timo? Are you down here, buddy?" Zion calls in a sing-songy voice.

naïs

Timo looks like an animal that's been cornered by its enemy. He's standing inside of an actual cage. A metal chain link wall that goes up to the ceiling. He's stuck. He can't run or escape, there is nowhere to hide.

"Timo Walsh?" Zion smiles. His excitement over what is about to happen is radiating off of him. "I think you know why we're here, yes?"

He gulps and nods, visibly shaking.

"Gideon Cross. I need to know everything that you know about his involvement in the attacks on my brother. We know that his cousin Marvin was involved... but we need more. We need concrete evidence that ties him to everything. Give us what we need and we all walk out of here happy." He casually looks at his nails. "We're also more than prepared to do this the hard way. Do you know what the hard way looks like, Timo?"

"I have something that you could use to blackmail him!" He

pulls a phone out of his pocket, fumbling it in his hands. "We don't need to do this the hard way!"

"Well, fuck me! I wasn't expecting this to be so easy. What have you got?" He steps forward toward the cage. Clint and I make surprised eye contact. I was preparing myself for carnage —for bloodshed and torture. This was painless.

"The phone is dead, but... this was my brother, Denny's. He was there at the attack. He didn't make it."

"Condolences. Why is that phone worth anything to us?" Zion narrows his eyes, showing absolutely no sympathy.

"About a year ago we did a...job for Mr. Cross. Marvin called, he wanted four of us to meet him at some swanky penthouse apartment. Umm.. when we got there, Denny secretly recorded a video because he was having some payment issues with Marvin. He was going to-"

"Let me stop you right there," Zion interrupts him. "Look, we really don't give a flying fuck about why he recorded the video. What's on it?"

"Umm, Mr. Cross... h-he needed us to dispose of a body." Timo looks like he's going to pass out at any moment.

The room goes completely silent. After a moment, I notice Zion's shoulders shaking. He snorts and bursts into a fit of uncontrollable laughter. Clint shakes his head and laughs too, less jovial and more skeptical.

"Please, continue," I nod, not finding the situation quite as funny as them.

"When we got to the apartment, there was a woman that Mr. Cross had killed... during sex. In the video, you can see him clearly, you can see her body and you can hear him screaming about killing her. It's incriminating."

Zion takes the phone and slips it into his pocket. "I'm going to take this home and pull up the video. If it isn't there, if it's not helpful if you're lying... I'm going to come back here. Do you know what I'm going to do?"

Timo nods his head, "no."

"I'm going to remove your fingers with pliers." Zion growls.

"I swear, it's there. It's just as I described it. You'll find it!" Timo visibly shakes.

"Clint, stay here with our friend. I'll call you as soon as I have the video." Zion places his hand on my shoulder and leads me out.

As soon as the door closes behind us, we stop, staring at each other in disbelief. Did that really just happen?

Grabbing my hand, he starts to run up the stairs two at a time, dragging me behind him. We burst through the door and passed Hanzo and his gross brother without a word. There's no time for talking. Not that I actually want to stop and talk to them.

"Take me to The Playground. My best equipment is there," he tells Declan as he pulls the phone out of his pocket and stares at it like it's going to start playing the video right now. "I'm going to need at least thirty minutes to break into it."

My knee bounces up and down nervously and my mind races. Once we have the video. Then what?

"Zion," I wonder out loud.

He hums and turns to me, I can see Declan watching from the front seat.

"I have an idea." By the time we reach The Playground, I've told them my scheme and they both stare at me with open mouths.

"Jesus Christ, remind me not to get on your bad side! That's perfect but first... we need the video." He jumps out and sprints inside.

Declan opens my door and walks with me into the club. It's weird here during the daytime. A few half-drunk men are scattered around, barely awake, watching the single dancer out on the stage.

We sit at the bar, silently, waiting for Zion. Declan pulls out his phone and starts to text, not paying the dancer any mind. I watch her for a moment before my eyes start to drift around the room. When they land on a specific spot on the stage, my cheeks burn.

Memories rush my brain, a flash flood of images that make me miss Kane so much that my eyes tear up. The look in his eyes, his hands on my body, the sounds he makes... each recollection is so vivid and real. It's as if his skin is touching mine right now. The fantasy plays over in my mind.

"Anaïs," he taps my shoulder.

"Huh?" I crash back down to reality.

At some point, Declan stood up, and I hadn't realized. "Zion is ready for us."

As we walk behind the bar and up the stairs to the office, I'm a bundle of nerves. Did he get the video? The huge smile on Zion's face eases any doubts.

"Holy shit," he excitedly starts the video.

I can hardly believe what I'm watching. Gideon, wearing only tighty-whitey underwear, is in a full-blown panic. Screaming about "getting rid of the body in The Underworld where no one will ever find it!" The girl is slumped over in the bed with a strange harness bunched up on her chest and neck. "It was an accident," he keeps saying, repeatedly. "Get her the fuck out of here!"

The hair on the back of my neck is standing straight up and goosebumps rise over my skin, sending a shiver down my spine.

"You ready for this?" Zion holds out the phone to me.

"I'm ready."

It's time yo get Kane out of there.

CHAPTER 30

 naïs

Jiji watches me pace back and forth, his eyes following me around the room.

This was the stupidest idea in the world. Why did I think I could do this?

"Kane," I whisper to myself. I'm doing this for Kane. Looking down at my jacket, I run my hands over it, smoothing it out. Oksana got me a three-piece suit, complete with vest and tie. If I'm going to channel Kane, I might as well go all the way.

"Anaïs!" Gideon strolls into the room, a notable pep in his step.

Jiji growls quietly beside me. "Go lay down," I snap my fingers.

"I'm sorry. All of this has been so difficult for you." He sighs, shaking his head as he sits at the conference table.

I bite into my tongue to keep myself from screaming. He

really is full of shit. All it took was one phone call and acting like I needed him. *"I can't do this, Gideon! I'm not cut out to lead The Underworld. Please, help me!"*

I knew he would come. He can't see past his ego to even consider that this is a setup. Taking a seat beside him, I try to hide the way his cologne makes my stomach roll. Now that I can see through the act, the fake exterior, I can't see anything else. He's physically attractive, but he's rotten on the inside, manipulative, and self-serving. He plays the part well, a concerned, helpful, benevolent leader up top... it's all lies.

"It's been so hard," I whimper. "I can't do this on my own." My eyes tear up, thinking about Kane sitting in that cell. I can't spend another night without him, crying into his pillow. This needs to end. Today.

"Don't worry, I'm here to help. I had paperwork drawn up. It only needs your signature. It gives me temporary authority to rule The Underworld." He slides a folder toward me.

"Or," I slide the folder back in front of him, "you could make the judgment right here, right now, that exonerates Kane of any and all wrongdoing in the self-defense killing of Cohen Farly."

He looks momentarily stunned, and then a smile spreads across his face. It's dark and ominous and makes my skin prick.

"Please tell me you didn't call me down here to beg for mercy..."

"I didn't," I cut him off. "I don't want mercy. I want you to drop the charges altogether." Sliding my phone across the table, "Call and have him released."

His face starts to turn red, a menacing look clouding his eyes. When he unexpectedly jumps up from his seat, I gasp and jerk back. His fists hit the table, rage clear in the hunched-over posture of his shoulders.

"Sign this fucking document, Anaïs, so help me God." His voice shakes, trembling with the fury that he's losing control over. For my own preservation, I slide away from him, standing and moving to the opposite side of the table.

"Before I sign that, I need you to see something that I believe will change your mind." I look toward the door. I know that Zion and Clint are waiting just on the other side, but I still feel very much alone. Declan is waiting at The Pits, ready to drive Kane away as soon as he is released.

Tapping the keyboard, the large television hanging on the wall moves from a black screen to the shaky start of the recording.

"What the fuck is-" the words die in his throat as he watches the video play. With each second, his eyes grow wider, bugging out of his head.

After the video plays, it restarts again. Zion set it on a loop that will continuously repeat until we stop it.

"Where did you get that?" He turns to me and my blood runs cold. If I thought he looked angry before... I was wrong. The man before me now is...terrifying. He looks like he's ready to pull the skin from my bones with his bare hands.

"That's not important. Make the call. Tell them to let Kane out, right now." I try to keep my posture tall, to not cower or show any fear. I have the upper hand here.

"Call, or this gets released, everywhere."

It feels like an eternity that we stand, staring at each other. He knows that defeated, but I can see the wheels turning in his mind, thinking through every possible scenario. Finally, he nods slightly and reaches for the phone.

"Warden Davies," a gruff voice comes through the phone.

"Davies, it's Cross. The judgment in the charges against Azrael is innocence, set him free effective immediately." He looks like he's going to be physically ill saying the words.

Whatever the warden replies, I don't hear it. My heart pounding in my ears blocks out everything else. He's being set free.

"I want this video erased. Every copy needs to be deleted...
where is Zion? I know he must be skulking around here
somewhere."

"You know that's not going to happen, Gideon. We're
keeping that evidence in case you...act up again." He can't really
think we will just hand over our leverage. His hubris knows no
bounds.

"Act up?" For some reason, this seems to enrage him more
than anything. "Give me the fucking video!" He screams at the
top of his lungs and jumps over the table. I'm stunned as he
grabs me by the neck, slamming my body into the window
behind me. Through the chaos, I vaguely register Zion bursting
through the door.

A loud, snarling bark cuts through his angry screaming as
Gideon is ripped away from my body. Jinx is on top of him,
biting anywhere and everywhere that he can sink his teeth. He
screams, attempting to crawl away.

Zion reaches me a second after, looking over me for
injuries.

"I'm fine," my voice shakes, but I really am alright. Jiji got to
him before he was able to do anything but press me into the
window.

"Goddamn," Clint mumbles over Gideon's screams. We all
stand motionless, watching Jiji rip him to shreds.

"Jinx," I whistle, and he stops immediately. Snapping my
fingers by my side, he runs to sit at my feet.

Zion grabs him by his arms, the shredded-up fabric of his
clothes revealing bite marks and broken skin. Knowing that
they have everything under control, I turn, running out of the
room as fast as I can.

The elevator ride to the lobby feels like it's taking so much
longer than it usually takes. My impatience grows by the
second. As soon as the doors open, I'm running through the
lobby and out the doors.

Searching the street, I see the car, maybe a block away.

The back door flies open and Kane jumps out. My breath catches, burning in my lungs as I start to sprint.

Our bodies collide painfully, bone meeting bone, but it doesn't matter. All that matters is his hands on my skin, running through my hair, holding me tightly to him.

CHAPTER 31

 naïs

WHEN WE PULL our mouths apart to take a breath, a small crowd has gathered around us in the street. I can't find it in me to care that they are watching. I feel flushed, but not from embarrassment. Holding him in my hands, feeling his arms wrapped around my body, I'm whole again.

His face is bruised, purple and blue streaking across his cheek below his eye.

"Declan told me about the recording and your plan," he pulls away only enough to be able to look at me. "Are you alright?"

"I am."

I run my hands over his chest. He's wearing a button-down shirt. He must have changed on the ride over. When I meet his eyes, he's looking at my clothes, too.

A smile tugs at the corners of his mouth. "What are you wearing?"

"A suit. Do you like it?"

"Baby," he groans, "you have no idea." He adjusts the front of his pants shamelessly.

"Can we go home?" I lean in to whisper into his ear.

He takes a step back and looks up, his eyes following the length of the building all the way to the top. "Yeah, fuck him, he can wait."

As soon as we're in the car, we're on each other, ripping at each other's clothes. I can't get him out of his shirt fast enough. His frantic movements match mine, yanking my pants down my legs.

Once we've pulled and ripped and torn away every barrier between us, he stops a sudden calm, relaxing his features. His fingers trace the tired lines under my eyes.

"I'm sorry, Anaïs. I know this week has been difficult, and you were out into a position that forced you to do things you didn't-"

Pressing one finger to his lips, I slide into his lap.

Once we're face to face, his exhausted eyes meeting mine, I position him against the ache between my legs.

He groans and presses the lock on the doors. In a moment of lucidity, I realize that we're in the parking garage at home already. Looking over my shoulder, I squint, searching for Declan through the smokey glass partition.

"He's gone."

With a grateful hum, I sink down, feeling him fill me the way that only he can. Not only my body, but my heart is brimming and ready to overflow.

"Don't apologize." The weight of how much I've missed him rises like quicksand, burying me alive. Hot, heavy tears spill down my cheeks as they have every night since he was taken into custody.

"Anaïs," his hands rake through my hair, holding the base of my skull, "I'm so sorry."

He doesn't understand.

"I'm…" a shuddering sob rips at my throat, forcing its way out over the words I'm trying to explain. I'm so relieved. Each day spent without him, I feigned confidence. Of *course,* we would find a way to free him. In the depths of my heart, though, I felt small and afraid. He's here. Our bodies are joined together, and the emptiness is so full now that it's overwhelming.

"I'll never forgive myself for the things you had to do and see, but I'm so proud of you. Queen of The Underworld." His eyes shine. I know he means it.

"I had to protect you."

Softness takes over his face. Something resembling a smile, only more filled with sadness than joy, spreads over his face. "Thank you."

Pressing my mouth to his, I let my lips tell him physically the feelings in my heart that I can't express with words. He returns the gesture with equal fervor. The temperature in the car is sweltering. Hot skin against skin, feverish mouths, hands roaming everywhere. I'm home. I feel peace down to my bones as the rolling boil of pleasure starts to build so rapidly that it takes my breath away.

"I missed you." His hands grip my hips, my waist, and my face. He leaves no skin uncaressed.

With the balmy air in my lungs and my head dizzy with lust, I roll my hips over him, sliding him out and then drawing him in again and again.

The deep rumble of his groans spurs me on.

Unrecognizable words and sounds spill past my lips as I reach the precipice. A sliver of a moment before pleasure takes over. Frozen in time with pressure so intense it's hard to take a breath.

"Kane," I choke on his name as my body leaps over the edge. I let go completely because I know he'll catch me.

His head falls back and his hands bite into my hips. With two hard thrusts, he follows me into the deep end of pleasure.

Sweaty and shaking, we hold each other until our breathing quiets enough to speak.

"Don't ever get arrested again," I nip at his neck.

"I'll do my best," his rumbling chuckle makes my stomach flutter. "How did things go with Gideon?"

"He demanded that I give him the recording and delete all copies in front of him..."

"I'm sure that arrogant son of a bitch actually thought he could demand that and you would do it. No person in their right mind would think that you would legitimately do it but him."

I know he's going to find out but I don't want to tell him, not yet. This moment is too perfect to ruin.

"He didn't try anything, did he?"

So much for that.

With a heavy sigh, I pull myself back enough to see his face. "He tried to attack me. Jiji got him before he could do anything and Zion was in the room a second after."

The silence makes me squirm until Kane sighs and drops his head down to my shoulder.

"There are a few things I haven't told you about Gideon."

Despite myself, I perk up. I have so many questions.

With his eyes pitched closed, he takes a deep breath. "My mother died when I was seven. Very quickly after, my father married Pamela Cross."

It takes my brain a moment to interpret all of the information he's sharing. I didn't know about his mom. Pamela Cross.

Cross.

"Cross as in Gideon?"

He hums, "Gideon became my stepbrother."

My mouth hangs open but no sound will come out, it's like a fist gripping my throat.

"Pamela hated us. We were living, breathing reminders of my dad's first wife. To please her, he cast us aside... Gideon was the golden child. My father ruled over all but when it came time for him to step down, he split the world between Gideon and I, leaving Zion with nothing."

I can't even believe what I'm hearing.

"K-Kane..." I don't even know where to begin. There isn't anything I can say.

"Don't cry for me, it was a long time ago." He wipes a tear from my cheek.

"It wasn't. You've only been ruler here for eight years, Kane."

"It's done." There is a finality in his voice that makes me close my mouth. He isn't ready to talk about this further or to hear that the way his father treated him wasn't his fault.

"It makes more sense why Gideon thought he would take over down here if you were out of the way..."

I think back over our conversations in the past. He always said 'We don't get along.' I wish I had known how deep that dislike went and how tangled everything really is.

"What are you going to do?" I run my fingers over the light stubble on his cheek.

"I'm going to kill him."

CHAPTER 32

ane

As soon as we climbed into bed, she fell asleep like someone who hadn't slept in weeks. She hasn't moved in hours. Not when I run my fingers over the delicate skin of her neck or when I kiss her hair. Each hour that passes, the more peaceful she looks.

I'm exhausted, but I don't want to sleep. The calm that I feel, settled into my bones is better than any sleep I've ever gotten. I don't want to stop touching her or watching her.

My phone buzzes quietly beside me, and I quickly open the message. Silencing the volume, I watch the video Zion attached. Even without sound, it's damning. There's no talking his way out of this.

Less than a second after it ends, my phone lights up. He's calling.

Sighing, I pull myself away from her sleeping body.

As I walk into the kitchen, I'm surprised to see him sitting at the counter, shirtless. Of course, he's shirtless, why would he have clothes on in my fucking house?

"What are you doing here?" I put the phone down.

"Are you kidding? I have so much pent-up frustration from not fucking him up that I had to release it somewhere." He sips a bottle of water. "Oksana passed out about an hour ago, I've been doing some digging." He slides his open laptop toward me.

The screen is open to the missing person database. "Rochelle Hosaka," I stare at the missing person's flyer. It could be the girl from the video but it's very difficult to tell.

"Look at the dates. She was last seen on January fourth of 2019, and the timestamp on the video is January fifth. She fits the physical description, hair length, color, and weight look about right..."

"Well, shit, it's definitely too much to be all coincidence."

"It gets better." His face morphs into that wicked smirk that he does so well. "He told the guys that she was an escort. You can even hear him saying it in the video. Rochelle Hosaka is the daughter of Senator Otani Yumiko. Definitely not an escort."

"What the fuck..."

"Maybe we give the senator a call?" He slides the phone toward me.

I hear the sound of water running in the distance, maybe the shower.

"Go ahead and call her team. If they want to see the video for themselves, send it. Tell them that if they want to bear witness to his punishment, they are welcome to meet us tomorrow in the judgment room."

"The judgment room? It's such sweet justice for that sack of shit to meet his end in The Pits." He almost whines.

"While I agree, I will never let Anaïs step foot in that place again."

His shoulders slump but he nods, "Alright. I get it. You should be proud of her, though, man. She was a badass."

"I am proud of her," I tell him over my shoulder as I quickly move back toward our room. I follow the dim light from the bathroom passed the empty bed.

Standing in the doorway, I watch as she pours something from a bottle into the bathwater. The curve of her waist, her hips, the slope of her back as it rounds into her perfect ass. I'm practically drooling.

"What are you doing?"

She yelps and spins around, clutching her chest. "You scared me! I was going to fill this up and come find you. Can I talk you into taking a bath with me?"

"Talk me into it? Try to keep me out of that tub."

The shining smile that spreads across her lips makes my heart beat painfully against my chest. Climbing into the warm water behind her, I let her back rest against me.

"Tomorrow is going to get ugly. I don't want to keep exposing you to this shit. I want your head filled with good things. These memories will haunt you."

"Do they haunt you?" She cranes her neck to look at me.

"No. What haunts me are all of the things that you have been exposed to. I know you're strong but your strength lies in your kindness, in the gentleness you can show to someone like me. I don't want to crush that with darkness."

"You can't protect me from everything. I'm your partner. If I'm going to stand beside you, I'm going to see it. I want to because you shouldn't have to shoulder it alone." Her fingers trace the bruises on my ribs.

"I don't want to harden the softness. Tainting you, ruining your spirit would be the worst thing I could do."

"You're not ruining anything. I'm here by choice." Her back straightens and a bit of an edge is clear in her soft voice.

I tried to control her before and it ended in my misery. I won't make that mistake again. This time, I'll go against my instincts to command.

"Zions here. I was talking to him when you woke up. We think he might have found the identity of the girl..." After telling her Zions' findings and our plan for tomorrow, she stands, stepping out of the bath.

"Where are you going?"

She turns, water running down her body, "if we're going to be surrounded by so much bad, I think we should probably fill up on love before we leave."

My cock has been hard against her back since we sat down. Now it's raging at full attention.

"Fuck me," I groan, jumping out after her.

"Oh, I plan to," she runs out of the room, leaving a trail of water on the floor behind her.

CHAPTER 33

 naïs

WHEN THE CAR comes to a stop outside of Kane's office, my hand instinctively tightens around his. A group of six men, surrounding a small woman, all in black, are standing to the side of the doors.

We're expecting more people than usual, but after last time, I can't stop the fear from creeping up my spine. He's not getting arrested...this is different. Taking a deep breath, I run my thumb over his hand, just to feel his skin.

"That's Senator Yumiko," Kane is watching her too.

As we approach the group their faces are stoic and emotionless, but the senator can't hide the redness around her eyes. I know she's been crying.

"Mr. Azrael, I would like to thank you for informing me of the evidence you found. I-" She stops and takes a deep breath. "I can confirm that my daughter is the one in that video."

"Cross will suffer," Kane tells her with a curt nod. There is a mutual respect between them that surprises me. After the revelation of his family history yesterday, I've been thinking over every interaction. People up top seem to fear him, but there isn't much respect there.

She lowers her head slightly, and they follow us into the lobby. In the elevator, Kane pulls me back to his chest, holding me across my chest with his arm. Even as we ride up to witness what I'm sure will be brutal and violent, I feel safe in his arms.

The clicking of our footsteps over the tile floor is the only sound, echoing off the walls. Inside the judgment room, Zion and Clint are standing on either side of Gideon. He's on his knees, his wrists chained to a metal ring bolted to the floor.

When he looks up, he pales, a visible tremble running through his body. He wasn't expecting to see Senator Yumiko here.

I watch the senator's hands clench by her sides and her jaw lock angrily as she stares at him down. He won't meet her eyes, but she isn't backing down.

"Unchain him," Kane's voice is completely calm.

I turn to him just as he shrugs his jacket off, laying it across his throne. When he starts to unbutton his shirt, I realize exactly what's about to happen. A knot burns in my throat. This is going to be even harder to watch than I thought.

With his shirt removed, he rolls his neck and clenches his fists.

When our eyes meet, I almost cower back. The sweet man who kissed every inch of my skin only a few hours ago is gone, replaced by a mountain of rage and muscle. He bends, his lips grazing my ear. "I love you."

Maybe not completely gone, just buried under his need for vengeance.

Reaching out to grip his shoulders, I pull him closer. "Please, don't get hit too much. I can't bear it."

The deep chuckle that I've grown to adore rumbles in his chest. "I won't get hit too much."

He turns, the broad muscles of his back tensing beneath his skin.

"Gideon Cross, for the crimes of murder and conspiring to commit murder, I find you guilty. Your sentence? Death." The calmness of his voice is chilling. "You may keep your wretched life if you will fight for it. Fight me, here and now, winner... lives."

I'm suddenly so cold that my teeth chatter. From the corner of my eye, I notice Declan inching closer to stand right behind me.

"He wouldn't do this if he didn't know he will win." He whispers so quietly that I barely hear it.

Without turning, I nod my head. He's right. Kane will win.

"Do you have any last words?"

Gideon is pulled up to his feet and pushed forward, sending him stumbling toward Kane. A menacing smile spreads across his face as he leans in, saying something that only Kane can hear.

It's like watching a switch flip. With my eyes locked on the man I love, I can see him change before my eyes. Years of anger and rage boil to the surface, overflowing in a whirlwind of fists, each connecting with Gideon's face.

Gideon falls back, rolling across the floor to put distance between them again. Kane moves, light on his feet, to the side until he's behind him. I'm shocked when Gideon spins, kicking his leg around so that his foot collides with Kane's ribs.

I don't know why it takes me completely by surprise that Gideon seems to have some training in hand-to-hand combat.

I quickly press my hand over my mouth, holding the gasp inside. I don't want to do anything that will distract Kane. Using his moment to full advantage, he spins around and lands two quick hits to Kane's face.

Kane spits blood onto the ground, blood dripping down his face from his now busted lip.

I have to pinch my eyes closed. Seeing him hurt is hard enough, seeing someone actually hitting him? I think I would rather take the hits myself...

A loud thud and the sickening crack of flesh and cartilage crunching force me to open my eyes. As much as I don't want to watch, I have to know what's happening.

Kane has him pinned to the floor, his fists raining down on him while he can only attempt to cover his face.

Gideon starts speaking, saying something muffled that I can't make out. Kane hears him though, and whatever he's saying, it's not good. Zion hears him too and starts to roll the sleeves up on his shirt. He's struggling to hold himself back from joining the fight.

"That might be true. He might not have loved me, but he didn't love you either. He showed you favor to appease your mother." Kane grits out through his clenched teeth before bringing his fists down against his face again.

My heart hurts for him. I'm acutely aware of how much it hurts to have your parent not love you. Gideon knows he's losing this fight so he's taking any last digs he can.

Shrinking back, I watch the droplets of blood. Every time Kane swings his arm down, they splatter across the floor. He hits Gideon until it looks like his arms are too heavy to lift.

Dragging himself up to his feet, he leaves Gideon's body on the floor. Tuning to Senator Yumiko, he wipes his bloody hands over his pants.

"He's not quite dead. You may take him. Do what you need to do to find peace."

A tear drips down her cheek as she reaches her hand out to shake his.

Careful not to touch me, he steps toward me. "Let's go, baby."

CHAPTER 34

ane

I KNOW that she wants to touch me. Her hands clench by her sides as we ride the elevator down to the lobby.

I can't let his blood get on her. I know she understands because she's forcing herself back. Pulling my shirt on, the material immediately sticks to my skin.

"What did he whisper to you before you hit him?" Her big blue eyes pierce into me, breaking me apart faster than any punch anyone could throw.

"I won't ever repeat it."

She nods, accepting that without hesitation. I can see the tension on her face. This day has been a lot for her. I want to pull her into my arms and comfort her.

"What happens now?"

"I'm going to shower and then feed you. You barely ate anything at breakfast this morning."

She rolls her eyes, but her lips twitch as she tries not to

smile. "I meant what happens with...everything. Who is going to rule up top now?"

"He must have someone named as his heir to the throne. If not, the Senate will probably vote. This has never happened before. I'm not sure what they will do."

When the car stops in the parking garage, she jumps out quickly, running around the back to the elevator. By the time I reach the elevator, she's already inside, holding the door open for me.

She's fidgety, rocking on her toes and picking at her fingers.

"Are you alright?"

"This is the slowest elevator..." she taps her toes against the floor.

When the doors slid open, she's rushing past me, straight down the hall.

"Anaïs," I jog after her, "what are you doing? Slow down."

She goes straight for the bathroom and starts the water in the shower.

"Please, please get in," her voice cracks. "I need to make sure you're alright. There is so much blood I can't even tell where you're actually hurt. I just want—I need to touch you."

I step under the spray in my clothes.

The water runs red as I strip out of the now-soaked fabric. Scrubbing my skin, I feel her before I see her. She's behind me in the shower, waiting. As soon as I'm clean, I turn to grab her, but she's faster than me. Her body launches into mine, holding me tightly against her.

Her lips press into my chest, leaving a trail of kisses over my skin. With gentle fingers, she studies each newly formed cut and bruise.

"You said you wouldn't get hit too much," she pouts, touching my cheek softly.

"I didn't. He hardly got any hits in!"

She scoffs and takes my hands in hers to look over my

busted knuckles. "We need to clean these with antibacterial spray. I want to wrap them up."

I bite back the groan that rises in my chest. I know from experience, she's not going to let that go, it's best just to let her do it.

She leads me to the counter, where she carefully concentrates all of her attention to each little mark. Her bottom lip is pulled between her teeth as she works.

Fuck.

When she's satisfied with the first aid she's administered, she steps back. "Does anything else hurt?"

"Yes."

Her eyes go wide with concern, "what? Is it your ribs? He kicked you so hard! You probably have fractures..." she turns, digging through the first aid bag.

"It's not my ribs."

She spins around just as I open the towel hanging at my hips.

She gasps, then scowls. "Kane! I'm being serious!"

"So am I. You're naked under your towel." Grabbing her hand, I press her palm against my cock.

When she squeezes me lightly, a groan vibrates in my throat.

"We had sex this morning," she looks up at me through her lashes.

"That was hours ago." I pull her forward and bury my face in her neck. She smells so good, soft and sweet. Her body presses forward, and I can feel her, the tension in her body releasing against me. Yesterday, last night, this morning... none of that matters. It's never enough. I want to live and die between her legs.

"Kane!" A loud banging from the bedroom door brings all of the tension back.

"Fucking Zion..."

WILL COME TO LIGHT

She giggles and steps out of my arms. "Go see what he wants. You know he won't go away until you do."

She's right. Fuck.

Pulling my towel closed, I stomp toward the door.

"What."

"Aww, man... were you guys fucking? My bad. We have some...visitors." He gestures down the hall.

"Here? In my house?" I choose to ignore the rest.

"You left the office and haven't answered your phone. What did you want me to do with them?" He shrugs.

"Bring them up to my home office. We'll be right there."

I wonder if we have time for a quickie before we meet them? They dropped in unannounced. It's not unreasonable to have them wait for ten minutes.

"Baby," I groan, "why are you getting dressed?"

"I heard you talking." She pulls a skirt up her legs that makes me want to drop to my knees.

"They can wait, fuck them," I pick her up, holding her body flush against mine. The pink that sweeps over her cheeks is more than I can take.

"Kane," she's breathless, "let's go. We'll see what they want, then spend the rest of the day in bed." She wiggles her body, sliding down over my aching cock to bring her feet back to the floor. When she's safely out of my reach, she turns, looking at me over her shoulder. "Don't pout, baby."

"I'm throwing them out after ten minutes," I rub my hand over cock and groan.

My pants are tight and uncomfortable as we walk to my office. She keeps 'accidentally' rubbing against me, her hand, her ass... she's trying to kill me.

Six senators are seated in my office, staring awkwardly at Zion.

"Let's make this quick, shall we? What do you want?" I pull a second chair behind my desk for Anaïs.

"We want you to be king, like your father and his father before him. Now that Gideon is gone, the Senate voted. We want you to take your rightful place as lord over all." One of them speaks.

Without a word, I stand, pulling Anaïs gently into the hallway with me.

"I don't want it," I take her face in my hands. "Do you want to be the queen overall? If you want it, we'll do it. When my dad ripped everything apart and gave Gideon the throne, none of them said a thing. In fact, most of them voted in favor of his motion to divide the kingdom. This feels like laziness. Finding someone is difficult, so they just want me to fill the slot."

"It's rightfully yours, Kane. You really don't want it? No matter why they are offering it… if you want it, you should take it." She watches me carefully.

"No."

"Then it's no from me too."

"You don't want to move up top and rule there?" I want her to fully understand what she's saying no to.

"Nope," she shakes her head, "if you don't want it, then I don't want it."

I search her face, looking for anything that would indicate that she actually wants to do this. I see nothing but genuine calm.

"Kane, if you wanted to go, I would go. I have absolutely no desire to be the queen up top."

When we re-enter the room, the senators look ready to congratulate us.

"No."

Zion snorts and sits up from the reclining position in his chair, clearly enjoying this.

"I'm sorry, did you say 'no'?" One of the senators speaks. All of their faces are completely shocked.

"Yes, No. We don't want it."

They turn to one another, mumbling and speaking quietly. "What about you Zion? Your birthright gives you the throne in the event that your brother abdicates."

Zion's head falls back, and a loud, joyous laugh fills the room. The senators shift in uncomfortable silence as he obnoxiously laughs for several minutes.

"Get fucked." He finally chokes out and they gasp. "When my father tore the kingdom apart and gave Gideon the throne up top over either of his own sons all of you sat by and watched. Now you're here because he turned out to be a murderer... no way. I don't want it."

"What are we supposed to do? This is unprecedented!" They're all in an uproar, talking over each other, rising to their feet. Panic.

"That's your problem. Now, if you would get the fuck out of my house, good day." I take Anaïs by her hand.

She blushes and mumbles a quiet 'goodbye' as I practically run out of the room.

CHAPTER 35

 naïs

Two Years Later

"Kane," I'm completely in awe. My eyes can't decide on a place to look. Everything is so perfect it doesn't seem real. The clear water, the trees, the rocky cliff that overlooks one side. A thin stream of water runs off the top, the pipeline of glacial water pouring fresh water down like a waterfall.

"Is it what you wanted?"

We're standing on the trail that circles the lake, looking out over the calm water. The orange sky looks less smoggy reflecting on the clear water.

"It's better than I ever imagined," I kick off my shoes to let my feet feel the soft dirt.

Taking his hand in mine, we walk behind a very excited Jinx. He runs into the water, then back to the trail, then back to the water.

"I can't wait for tomorrow! It was starting to feel like this was never going to be completed. I'm so excited for everyone to see it." I feel bouncy anticipation all the way down to my toes.

"Have you decided what you want to name the lake?" He nods toward the blank sign.

"No. I don't know why it feels like such a big responsibility. It took two years to build this lake. I want the name to be meaningful. Zion wants to call it Lake Oksana."

He chuckles. "That's weird."

"I think it's sweet."

"Zion isn't sweet. If he's suggesting it, there's definitely more to it." He pulls me so that I'm walking with my back to his chest.

As we round the curve of the trail, a blanket spread out on the water's edge catches my eye.

"What is that?" There is a basket on the ground beside the blanket.

"Lunch." He wraps his arms around my chest, holding me to him as we walk clumsily toward the picnic.

"When did you plan this?" I look around for Declan. He must be close by. I'm sure he set this up.

The basket holds champagne, sliced fruits, and chocolate dip.

"Are you trying to seduce me, Kane Azrael?"

"Always," he flashes one of the rare smiles that makes my stomach flutter and my heart constrict. I see them more often than I used to, but they still make me sweat.

Removing his jacket, he lies on his back beside me, his arms folded behind his head. There is a peace about him now that shows itself more and more. With his eyes closed and his body relaxed, he hums slightly. I don't recognize the song, but I nod my head along with the catchy tune.

"Bite," I hold a slice of strawberry dipped in chocolate to his lips.

Without opening his eyes, he opens his mouth, smiling as I

feed him. Jiji finally gets tired of darting all over the trail and comes to curl his body beside Kane on the blanket.

When most of the fruit is gone, I stretch out across the blanket, laying my head on his chest.

"I've been thinking about my mom lately," he mentions casually.

"You have? What about her?" I'm surprised that he's bringing her up. It took almost a year for him to open up and talk about her. Emily Azrael.

"She would have liked you."

"I wish I could have met her."

He hums and brings his hand up, the pad of his thumb softly grazing my lower lip.

"I love you very much," he says quietly.

Bringing my hand under my chin, I roll onto my stomach so I can see his face.

"I love you."

He reaches out to run his fingers through my hair. "Will you be my wife?"

I sit up, shocked. Surely, I misheard him. He couldn't have said what I think I heard. Not with that calm look on his face.

"What?"

A boyish, lopsided smile spreads across his face as he digs into the pocket of his pants. A small red box sits in his outstretched hand, waiting for me to take it.

"Kane..."

"Open it," he's still smiling.

With trembling fingers, I take the box and snap it open. The metal is shaped into an intricate flower with a large, light green gemstone in the center.

"This is gorgeous."

Pulling himself to sit, he takes the ring out of the box, holding it between his fingers. "Try it on."

The ring slides onto my finger with ease and my breath catches in my throat.

"It belonged to my mom."

I can't take my eyes off of it. I know he doesn't have anything left to remember her. It's hard to believe that he would give this away.

"After he married Paula, he gave her all of Mom's jewelry." He takes my hand, kissing the tips of my fingers. "I don't know the history of that ring. I just know that it was one that my mom never took off. I remember it on her finger. I snuck into their room and stole it from the jewelry box." He chuckles at the memory. "They punished Zion and me for weeks, but I had it hidden where they would never find it. I didn't think I would ever want to give it to anyone. I just didn't want Paula to have it. It would be the greatest honor of my life if you would wear it... if you would be my wife."

Tears drip down my cheeks. I want to jump up and down, to scream from the top of the cliff for everyone in The Underworld to hear but I'm so overwhelmed that I only choke on a sob.

"Are those 'yes' tears or 'no' tears?" He chuckles nervously.

"Yes tears," I lunge forward, grabbing his face in my hands. "I really want to be your wife."

The warm, wet kiss that seems to last forever feels different than the countless kisses shared over the past two and a half years. It's deeper, connected in a way that feels eternal.

"What about Emily Azrael Memorial Lake?" I pant breathlessly against his lips.

"Sounds like a good place for her grandchildren to grow up," he grinds his hips up against me.

A burst of laughter bubbles up in my throat. "I guess it does."

165

BONUS CHAPTER

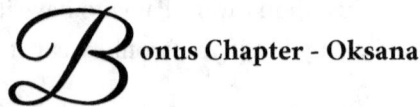

onus Chapter - Oksana

I CAN'T KEEP STILL. The anticipation of what's about to happen has me uncomfortably wet.

What is taking him so long?

The elevator dings and I nearly jump out of my skin. A momentary panic grips me. What if it's not him? Everyone is busy right now but what if something came up? What if they're home early?

I have less than a split second to do anything. It's not like I can hide now. Opting to just go with it, I put my hand on my hip, waiting for whoever steps out.

He freezes mid-step, halfway out of the elevator.

"Jesus Christ, Oksana. Are you trying to kill me?" He groans.

I feel my cheeks heat. That was definitely the reaction I was hoping for.

The red lace panties and matching garter are connected to

red fishnet stockings. I went with no top. He stares at my tits every chance he gets. I figured I would remove any obstacles.

In a few long strides, he's pressed flush against me. His hand wraps around the back of my neck, gripping me tightly as he slams our mouths together. Fuck, he tastes good. His kiss is bruising, forcing his tongue into my mouth, claiming it as his, at least for the night.

When I invited him over, I was expecting sex. We've danced around it for a while, we both want it. I still wasn't sure what to expect, though. This is exactly what I wanted. Raw, passionate, desperation.

With his free hand, he kneads my chest roughly, massaging me, and pinching my nipples. His rough hands feel better than I imagined they would.

"I've fantasized about fucking you since the day we met," he groans against my mouth.

"Me too."

In a sudden burst of movement, he has me on the ground, his body over mine. I can feel him, rock hard, pressed into my stomach. I yank at his shirt. I want him naked. He stands, leaving me sitting on the ground before him.

His tattooed skin ripples over taut muscles. Fuck. I really do have a type.

When he pulls his pants down, and his huge cock falls out, I almost choke. The geometric shapes tattooed on his stomach continue down into his dick.

"Holy shit, Clint!" I grab him, ignoring his strained grunt, and study the intricate details. "How the fuck did you do this?"

A cocky smirk pulls at his lips. "Do you like it?"

Instead of answering, I run the tip of my tongue over his shaft. He moans a deep raspy sound that has me dripping.

Pulling myself up onto my knees, I suck him into my mouth. Looking up at him, I stare him in the eyes as I slowly move up, taking him all the way. When I swallow, pulling him down into my throat, he loses it.

"Oh, my- how the fuck?" He groans loudly. His hips pump forward slowly. He's struggling to keep his eyes open. Every time I swallow or moan, they roll back and flutter closed. His hand is threaded into my hair, holding me so tightly against my scalp that my skin burns.

His hips thrust forward, pushing himself into my mouth faster. Spit runs out of my mouth, dripping down my chin onto the floor.

I'm so turned on I would drown him if he put his face between my legs.

Relaxing my throat further, I hum, letting the vibrations from my vocal cords ripple against his cock. The sound that comes out of him is so desperate it causes goosebumps to prick at my skin.

"Oksana," he grunts into the air, "I'm about to-"

I reach up and squeeze his balls gently. Cum shoots down my throat and he pulses against my tongue. His hand holds my head still as he empties himself completely into my mouth.

When he releases me, I slide back, letting him fall out of my mouth with a 'pop.'

For a moment, no one moves, we just stare at each other breathlessly.

"Stand up and turn around," his voice is gruff. He's definitely not asking.

As I stand, he drops to his knees behind me. "Grab your ankles," he grunts.

Well, shit.

As soon as I'm bent over, his hands run up the back of my legs. I feel his fingers against the thin strip of fabric of my panties for a moment before he continues up to touch my ass. It's softer than I was expecting.

Hums of approval from deep in his throat make me squirm.

"Clint, please," I groan. The pulsating nerves between my legs are becoming too much to take.

His fingers pull my soaked thong to the side. I gasp as his breath hits my throbbing clit. With a tight grip, he grabs my ass, opening me up for him. My pussy is so needy for attention that I whimper. If he doesn't do something soon, I'm going to have to use my fingers.

"You're dripping," his voice is gravelly. "Did sucking my cock get you all worked up?"

He's teasing now, but just a moment ago he was the desperate one.

Before I can answer, his face is pressed exactly where I need it. He licks and sucks at me, moving his tongue quickly. Each lick brings me higher.

"Oh, my god..." I'm breathless as he slurps and sucks me into a frenzy.

I teeter on my feet as two of his fingers unexpectedly slide into me. When his tongue sweeps over my ass while his fingers massage me, I brace myself. My legs shake.

"Fuck, Clint," I scream, dropping my hands to the ground in front of me for support.

Something like a moan and a sob rips from my throat as I come against his relentless fingers. Through my scream, I vaguely hear another sound.

"What the fuck?"

Zion's booming voice cuts through the post-orgasmic bliss that makes me feel like I'm floating.

Clint grips my hips, keeping me upright as I meet Zion's face. He's flushed, panting, and...angry. He's standing in front of the elevator, frozen. When I look down, I can see the bulge in the front of his pants.

"Zion?" I call after him as he turns on his heels and marches back into the elevator.

When the doors slide closed, I turn to Clint, who looks as confused as I feel.

"What the fuck was that?"

"I'm not sure." I can't help but start to laugh. We just got caught with his head up my ass.

He laughs too; the sound reminds me why he's here in the first place.

"Maybe we should take this to my bedroom."

A NOTE FROM THE AUTHOR

Dear Reader,

I wanted to take this opportunity to thank you. Writing books is my dream, and knowing that you've taken the time to read them means everything to me. I can't express enough how grateful I am for your support. If you enjoyed the story, it would mean the world if you left a review on Amazon or Goodreads. Your thoughts help other readers discover the book. Even a few words make a huge difference! If you're not able to, that's okay —I'm just happy you're here. Thank you for being a part of this journey with me. I appreciate you more than you know.

With gratitude,

Myranda

ALSO BY MYRANDA RAE

Contemporary

When I Whisper His Name

Unplanned

Lewd & Lascivious

The Void He Fills

Pink

Paranormal/Shifter

Beast

Hardest to Love

Alphas, Kings & Playthings

www.ingramcontent.com/pod-product-compliance
Lightning Source LLC
Chambersburg PA
CBHW071914220626
47052CB00002B/348